HOMETOWN HEARTS

SHIPMENT 1
Stranger in Town by Brenda Novak
Baby's First Homecoming by Cathy McDavid
Her Surprise Hero by Abby Gaines
A Mother's Homecoming by Tanya Michaels
A Firefighter in the Family by Trish Milburn
Tempted by a Texan by Mindy Neff

SHIPMENT 2
It Takes a Family by Victoria Pade
The Sheriff of Heartbreak County by Kathleen Creighton
A Hometown Boy by Janice Kay Johnson
The Renegade Cowboy Returns by Tina Leonard
Unexpected Bride by Lisa Childs
Accidental Hero by Loralee Lillibridge

SHIPMENT 3
An Unlikely Mommy by Tanya Michaels
Single Dad Sheriff by Lisa Childs
In Protective Custody by Beth Cornelison
Cowboy to the Rescue by Trish Milburn
The Ranch She Left Behind by Kathleen O'Brien
Most Wanted Woman by Maggie Price
A Weaver Wedding by Allison Leigh

SHIPMENT 4
A Better Man by Emilie Rose
Daddy Protector by Jacqueline Diamond
The Road to Bayou Bridge by Liz Talley
Fully Engaged by Catherine Mann
The Cowboy's Secret Son by Trish Milburn
A Husband's Watch by Karen Templeton

SHIPMENT 5

His Best Friend's Baby by Molly O'Keefe
Caleb's Bride by Wendy Warren
Her Sister's Secret Life by Pamela Toth
Lori's Little Secret by Christine Rimmer
High-Stakes Bride by Fiona Brand
Hometown Honey by Kara Lennox

SHIPMENT 6

Reining in the Rancher by Karen Templeton
A Man to Rely On by Cindi Myers
Your Ranch or Mine? by Cindy Kirk
Mother in Training by Marie Ferrarella
A Baby for the Bachelor by Victoria Pade
The One She Left Behind by Kristi Gold
Her Son's Hero by Vicki Essex

SHIPMENT 7

Once and Again by Brenda Harlen
Her Sister's Fiancé by Teresa Hill
Family at Stake by Molly O'Keefe
Adding Up to Marriage by Karen Templeton
Bachelor Dad by Roxann Delaney
It's That Time of Year by Christine Wenger

SHIPMENT 8

The Rancher's Christmas Princess by Christine Rimmer
Their Baby Miracle by Lillian Darcy
Mad About Max by Penny McCusker
No Ordinary Joe by Michelle Celmer
The Soldier's Baby Bargain by Beth Kery
The Maverick's Christmas Baby by Victoria Pade

HOMETOWN HEARTS

It's That Time of Year

CHRISTINE WENGER

◆HARLEQUIN® HOMETOWN HEARTS

Recycling programs
for this product may
not exist in your area.

ISBN-13: 978-0-373-21494-5

It's That Time of Year

Printed in U.S.A.

www.Harlequin.com

Christine Wenger has worked in the criminal justice field for more years than she cares to remember, but now spends her time reading, writing and seeing the sights in our beautiful world. A native central New Yorker, she loves watching professional bull riding and rodeo with her favorite cowboy, her husband, Jim. You can reach Chris at PO Box 1823, Cicero, NY 13039, or through her website at christinewenger.com.

To the dedicated staff and retirees of the Onondaga County Probation Department in Syracuse, New York. Thanks for the friendship, the support and the great ride. Be careful out there!

And to Gayle Callen, outstanding writer and wonderful friend! Thanks for everything, Gayle!

Chapter One

"When is this going to be over?" Melanie Bennett mumbled to herself as she adjusted her thick woolen mittens. If one more person shook her hand, hugged her or pressed a cold-lipped kiss to her frozen cheeks, she was going to scream.

It was the Saturday after Thanksgiving and the entire population of Hawk's Lake had turned out for the lighting of the Christmas tree, the traditional kickoff to the annual Snow Festival. This year Melanie and her son, Kyle, would be lighting the tree in her husband's memory.

She was grateful for everyone's support, but

she didn't want to talk about Mike anymore. It was too hard trying *not* to remember.

And she dreaded having to be in such close proximity to Samuel LeDoux, former Canadian hockey star and alleged expert in disaster recovery operatives for the Red Cross.

Unfortunately for her, Mayor Lippert had asked him to be the grand marshal of the Snow Festival. He was the overwhelming favorite, because he'd helped out during the horrific ice storm that had hit upstate New York last winter, and everyone in the village thought Sam LeDoux was a hero.

Everyone except her.

Someone jostled Melanie, and then she in turn bumped into someone else. Out of the corner of her eye, she saw a white foam cup flip in the air and hit the ground. When she looked up, she saw wisps of steam rising from a dark stain on the front of the red parka of the attractive man next to her.

"Oh, I'm terribly sorry. I made you drop your coffee." She pulled off a mitten, found a tissue in the pocket of her jacket and began blotting his parka. He looked down at her in amusement, his blue eyes twinkling.

And immediately she felt drawn to him.

Melanie could barely think. She was busy

looking at his strong jaw with a hint of a beard, and the tan that made his teeth look whiter. His lips formed a perfect smile, and she could tell he was in excellent shape in spite of the bulky parka.

She dropped her hand before she wore a hole through him. "Sorry. It's the mother in me. I'm used to wiping up spills on an hourly basis." Her face flamed in spite of the freezing temperatures.

"No harm done." He chuckled. "It'll dry, and it'll wash out." His deep voice, with a hint of an accent, enveloped her like a warm blanket. "Big crowd here, isn't there?"

"I've never seen so many people in Hawk's Lake at one time. Must be a record."

The stranger bent over to pick up the cup just as a Boy Scout appeared holding out a trash bag. He tossed it in.

"I'm going to get another cup of coffee," he said. "Would you like anything?"

"It's on me," Melanie shouted, as the six-piece band from Moose Lodge #814 played a much too loud and painfully slow rendition of "Jingle Bells." The crowd huddled around the white octagonal bandstand burst into song, making it even harder to carry on a conversation. And for whatever reason, she wanted to talk to him more.

She reached into her pocket and pulled out a dollar bill. He shook his head, leaned over and spoke into her ear, "It was nice bumping into you. Maybe I'll get to talk to you later."

She nodded, trying to calm her racing heart. The warmth of his breath on her skin made her shiver. She told herself she was only nervous about the upcoming tree lighting, but she knew it was more than that. She wanted to get to know the handsome stranger.

Watching as he walked away, she couldn't help but notice his butt, encased in snug dark jeans that outlined his muscular legs. She saw him wave to people and then stop to shake hands with others before he disappeared into the gingerbread tent.

How did he know so many people from Hawk's Lake? She'd lived here all her life and had never seen him before. She'd assumed he was a tourist who had come in for the Snow Festival.

To distract herself, she looked up at the bright stars sparkling in the black winter sky. They looked close enough to touch. When she was a little girl, her mother used to tell her that each star was a light for the people in heaven so they could see their way at night.

She grimaced. If that was true, her late husband Mike was plugged in to the nearest star watching a college football game and scouting for the next sensational player.

Kyle appeared at Melanie's side. She looked down at him and smiled tenderly. He'd been only five when his father had died in the devastating ice storm that had hit all of upstate New York a year ago.

Kyle grinned up at her. "When do we get to light the tree, Mom?"

"Pretty soon."

Yesterday, she had explained to him that this year's tree lighting was in honor of his father and it was a special way for the people of Hawk's Lake to remember him and to thank him for helping out in the storm.

Kyle had simply said, "But we remember him all the time, and Daddy shouldn't have gone out in bad weather."

True on both counts.

"I miss him. I'm going to ask Santa Claus to bring him back." And then Kyle had cried—something he rarely did.

It had been all Melanie could do to keep from crying for her son. How would they ever get through this Christmas with Kyle missing his father so much? Even thinking about it now threatened to bring tears to her eyes.

She was so angry at Mike. And although she still had difficulty remembering all the details of the storm, she knew that she couldn't bring herself to forgive him. Something was holding her back.

Last year, she'd spent the holidays in a hazy state of shock. Her father had told her that she'd slipped and fallen on the ice, but she only remembered waking up in the emergency room. Later she'd learned that Mike had died while helping to cut trees away from the power station, and that Sam LeDoux, a disaster response expert for the Red Cross, had stepped in to manage the volunteers, as well as the cleanup and recovery effort.

As far as *she* was concerned, he had done a horrible job of managing the volunteers.

But she had a son to think of, and this year, things would be different. She had to make this Christmas special for Kyle, to show him that it was okay to move on.

Melanie looked around, trying to spot the handsome stranger again, but he was lost in the crowd.

The villagers were holding lighted red candles pushed through holes in the bottom of waxed cups. Others held their children's hands and swayed with the music as the Moose Lodge Band jauntily played "Rudolph the Red-Nosed Reindeer." The frosty breath of the crowd hung in the air like smoke.

She figured that the increase in attendance had a little to do with Mike, but it probably had just as much to do with the grand opening of the new Santa Claus House, directly across from the bandstand on the east end of the square.

Santa's House was her father's brainstorm. Ed Hawkins had designed the little cottage, and Melanie and her two brothers had built it in their spare time in the back of their garage.

Melanie had painted the house a bright white and the gingerbread trim in Christmas red and forest green. Later, Santa Claus—played by her brother Jack—would sit on the porch of the bright little cabin on a regal chair that used to belong to their aunt Betty, and listen to the kids' wishes. Jack loved Santa duty, probably because he was still a kid at heart himself.

But the house was more than a labor of love for all the children in the village to enjoy—it was therapeutic for her, too. With each brush stroke, she'd thought that if not for her family, Kyle wouldn't have had any Christmas at all.

She shook her head, straightened her shoulders. No more sadness, she reminded herself. It was time to move on, and the first step was to make Christmas a happy time again.

Leading Kyle toward the bandstand, Melanie turned her attention to the bronze statue of her stern great-great-grandfather Ezra Packard Hawkins, standing proudly in the middle of the square. Ezra had founded Hawk's Lake in 1865, opening a smithy when his horse threw a shoe.

Ezra looked about as happy as she felt.

The chairman of the tree-lighting event took her hand and Kyle's. They were both shuttled up the steps and onto the bandstand. There she saw the mayor, Calvin Lippert, standing with... *him*.

The handsome stranger. The man she'd been admiring. That unsettling warmth flooded her veins again.

Mayor Lippert gestured for her to come closer. "Melanie Bennett, I'd like you to meet Sam LeDoux."

The instant warmth turned into a chill that went right to her bones. *This* was Sam LeDoux? The man responsible for Mike's death?

And she'd been attracted to him!

LeDoux raised a black eyebrow. "Melanie Bennett?" He looked just as shocked as she felt.

LeDoux's gaze met hers and she thought she saw a touch of sympathy in his dark blue eyes. Well, she didn't want his sympathy. Sympathy wouldn't bring her son's father back. Disappointed, she looked away, and then moved to Cal's other side with Kyle. The whole village would probably shun her for snubbing LeDoux, but she didn't really care.

As the mayor addressed the crowd, she searched for her family so she wouldn't have to look at LeDoux.

She spotted Jack with his latest girlfriend clinging to him like a piece of lint. He smiled at Melanie and gave her a thumbs-up for support. Her brother attracted women like this elevation attracted snow, and Melanie had given up trying to remember their names.

Next to Jack was their older brother, Brian. He met her gaze and sent her an encouraging nod. He was the most serious of the Hawkins clan.

Standing next to Brian was her father. He just smiled and winked at her. Ed didn't do serious very well.

Melanie swallowed the lump in her throat and squeezed Kyle's hand. They were her family. In good times and in bad, the descendants of old Ezra Packard Hawkins were always there for each other—meddling in one another's lives, of course.

As Mayor Lippert rambled on, she couldn't help but steal a glance at Sam LeDoux. He was looking at her again. She frowned. He arched a perfect black eyebrow.

She hated that she found him attractive, with his pitch-black hair and blue eyes and the masculine way he stood with his hands in the pocket of his jeans. His now coffee stained coat was open, as if the cold didn't even bother him.

He brought her conflicted feelings to the surface—anger, hurt, loneliness and more than a little guilt. Feelings she'd successfully buried for a year.

She shivered in the frigid mountain air when she caught a bit of Cal's speech. "Mike Bennett was a good father and a good neighbor, and could always be counted on to do the right thing."

The right thing.

She and Mike had married when she'd become pregnant with Kyle. It had seemed right at the time. Their brief marriage had been comfortable for the most part, but in truth they'd both been far from content.

She heard Mayor Lippert's voice grow louder. "Now, ladies and gentlemen, without further ado, please give a warm Hawk's Lake welcome to the grand marshal of our Snow Festival, Mr. Samuel LeDoux. Let's hear it for Sam!"

A cheer went up from the crowd as Cal handed LeDoux the microphone. Sam looked at it for a moment as if deciding what to do. The crowd grew silent. Melanie's stomach churned. She didn't want to hear a thing he had to say.

"Thank you for inviting me to this wonderful event. I'm honored to be here." His voice was deep and it vibrated clear down to her toes. "But I have to disagree with Mayor Lippert. I am not a hero. Mike Bennett was the hero that day."

LeDoux handed the microphone back to the mayor as the crowd applauded.

Cal passed Melanie the microphone, and she tried to protest, but he wouldn't hear of it. Her mind went blank for what seemed like an eternity, and then she tried to find the words, the right words.

She wouldn't say what she wanted to LeDoux. She wouldn't ruin this event for everyone, especially Kyle.

Melanie took a deep breath. "I'd like to thank everyone for coming and remembering Mike. Kyle and I appreciate your support." Her voice was quivering, and she swept her red mittens across her cheeks to wipe away her tears. "Thank you so much. Merry Christmas!"

The mayor guided the three of them to a red-ribboned pillar. On the pillar was a metal button that, she assumed, would light the tree.

Melanie positioned Kyle between herself and Samuel LeDoux.

As the Hawk's Lake High School marching band struck up "O Christmas Tree," Marylou Lang from the *Adirondack Sentinel* approached the bandstand, gesturing for the three of them to pose with the mayor for a picture. Then she wanted more pictures of Melanie, Kyle and Sam with their hands poised above the light switch.

"Closer." Marylou waved her hand as she looked through her camera. "No. That won't do. Closer. Melanie, take your mittens off and all of you put your hands on top of one another's on the button."

Kyle's hand already hovered over the button. Melanie yanked her mitten off, pasted a smile on her face, and placed her hand over Kyle's.

Her heart did a little flip as LeDoux's warm hand closed over hers. He was too close. His aftershave drifted around her, a light cloud of spice and pine. Her mouth suddenly went dry. She didn't want to feel the warmth of his hand,

and she didn't want to see his frosty breath mingle with hers.

She wanted him out of Hawk's Lake.

Take the picture, Marylou.

In the background, the village counted down. "Four…three…two…one…"

"Wow!" Kyle shouted as they all clamped down on the switch. Hundreds of bright colored lights illuminated the huge Douglas fir as the crowd cheered.

All Melanie could think of was getting away from there. Away from her thoughts. Away from Sam LeDoux, and this awareness of him that she couldn't tamp into submission.

Melanie slipped her hand back into her mitten. In less than five seconds, she was down the steps of the bandstand and heading for her car with her son in tow.

"Mrs. Bennett, please wait!"

It was LeDoux. Oh, *why* couldn't he have stayed in Canada?

"Mom! Wait! I have to talk to Santa!"

It was finally Kyle's voice that penetrated the red haze in her mind. What was she doing?

She hunkered down in front of Kyle. His eyes were wide and his nose red from the cold. "Okay, honey. We'll go and see Santa."

He relaxed and she stood up. Walking toward

them was her brother Brian, looking puzzled. Sam LeDoux had stopped beside her, still too close for comfort.

"I was wondering why you were leaving so quickly when Santa's coming to town," Brian said to her. Turning toward LeDoux, Brian held out his hand. "Good to see you again, Sam."

"Same here, Brian."

They shook hands, and Brian looked from Melanie to Sam and back again. Brian must have noticed the tension between them, because he gave a slight smile.

She could handle LeDoux herself, darn it. Besides, after they'd all worked with him last year, her whole family sang his praises, Brian included, so they weren't likely to agree with her feelings. She'd just keep silent and let her negative thoughts churn inside her.

Grand marshal or not, she wanted him gone. He was a reminder of her past, when she just wanted to focus on the future.

She smiled at Kyle. "Sweetie, how about if Uncle Brian takes you for some cocoa and cookies at the gingerbread tent? Then we'll get in line to see Santa." She turned to her brother. "Would you mind?"

"Not at all."

"Cool," said Kyle. Brian led him away, leaving Melanie alone with LeDoux.

Suddenly, she wanted to run as far away as her clunky boots would take her. He was too big, too real, making her think of him in ways she didn't want to.

"Could we talk for a minute?" he asked.

Her voice shook. "I'm sorry, Mr. LeDoux, I'd rather not."

"But I—"

"No. There isn't anything for us to talk about, and it's been quite an emotional night already." The words hung in the air between them like icicles. "Goodbye, Mr. LeDoux."

Chapter Two

"Wait! Mrs. Bennett… Melanie." Sam jogged after her. He didn't want to scare her. She already looked at him as if he carried some contagious disease.

She turned toward him, fire in her eyes. Her blond hair did a soft dance in the winter breeze. Her cheeks had a flush of color, either from the cold or from anger—most likely both.

The evening had started out so nicely when they'd first met, he'd seen the interest in her eyes, and he had felt the same awareness of her. Then the interest faded when she'd heard his name.

Sam knew darn well that everyone in Hawk's

Lake thought he was a hero—except Melanie Bennett. Well, he didn't think so, either. He wanted to forget the past just as badly as she did.

But the only way he could forget the past—and himself—was to discuss it, and she didn't want to do that.

"I'd like to somehow start over with you," Sam said.

"Unless you can turn back the clock, that's not possible. Just enjoy being Hawk's Lake's hero."

He shook his head. "I'm not a hero. I was only doing my job."

"Well, you didn't do it very well, did you?"

Her words—and the pain in her voice—pierced his heart. Sam wished she'd at least let him apologize, let him explain. But how could he do that without casting a shadow over the memory of her husband?

Damn the timing of that ice storm. Another place, another time, and Sam would never have known that the Bennetts even existed. He would have simply answered the call from the Red Cross and hopped on a plane, ready for action.

Instead, last year he had flown in for the christening of Cal Lippert's son, so he was already in tiny Hawk's Lake in the middle of the

Adirondack Mountains when the Red Cross called. As it turned out, he was in the perfect place to help.

That ice storm had changed his life forever.

Melanie glanced toward the crowded gingerbread tent as Sam fought the urge to grab her hand and escort her to some private place where she could yell at him until she was exhausted.

There wasn't anything that she could say to him that he hadn't already told himself.

But if it was all out in the open, maybe then he could find some peace.

He tried again. "Would you mind if we went somewhere private to talk?"

"My son wants to see Santa." She turned and walked away without a goodbye.

He didn't try to stop her this time.

With a sigh, he tried to focus on the moment, on the sights and sounds of the celebration around him. But all too soon the memories would surface again, knotting his stomach, and he'd question his judgment once again.

He couldn't direct a crew or manage an operation when he couldn't trust his instincts. It was too dangerous. Not for him, but for the volunteers— brave men and women who trusted him, who put their lives into his hands.

Hands that now shook with hesitation and indecision.

If he was honest with himself, Sam didn't know what he could accomplish by talking to Melanie. Maybe he wanted her forgiveness for his damn stupid mistake so he could function as a manager again.

Maybe then he'd get the peace he craved.

Sam felt like a fraud. When he had received the invitation a month ago, he'd phoned his old hockey buddy Cal Lippert and insisted that he had no right to light the Hawk's Lake Christmas tree, or to be their grand marshal for the three weeks of the Snow Festival.

"The hell you don't, Sam," Cal had said. "The whole town was grateful that the best emergency relief manager in the Red Cross was right here when that storm hit. We'd probably still be trying to bail out if it wasn't for you."

"A man died, Cal. I should have told Mike Bennett to get out of that tree earlier. Matter of fact, I never should have let him get up there in the first place."

"Things happen."

"Not on my watch."

"Yes, Sam, even on your watch. No one blames you."

Cal wouldn't take no for an answer, so here he was in Hawk's Lake. Again.

But returning to Hawk's Lake was a good opportunity to meet Melanie, apologize, and make sure that she and Kyle were doing okay after losing Mike.

Last year, he hadn't had the opportunity. He'd been in the hospital recovering from hypothermia. After he was discharged and wanted to call on her, her father, Ed, had told him that Melanie had suffered a concussion along with some amnesia and that her doctor had told everyone to wait for her memory to return before discussing the traumatic events.

But he'd had to leave soon after and never did get to see her or Kyle. Other disasters—fires, floods—had beckoned.

Sam leaned against a thick maple tree and watched Melanie and Kyle in the line waiting for Santa. They seemed like they were doing okay, considering everything. They were smiling and laughing at a man dressed in a reindeer costume juggling candy canes. The juggler lost more than he could keep in the air and eventually resorted to just handing them out.

Older children wearing angel costumes over their snowsuits were passing out cookies and ribbon candy.

Hawk's Lake was a wonderful place. It reminded Sam of the small Canadian town where he'd grown up. On the north shore of Lake Ontario, Lenore had once been a quiet, beautiful town where everyone knew everyone else.

But everything changed—even little Lenore.

"Enjoying yourself?"

Sam took the cup of coffee that Cal handed him, grateful that his friend seemed content to make small talk. As soon as he drained the last drop, a tiny, curly-haired girl dressed as an angel appeared to take his cup and offer him some cookies. He chose a frosted one in the shape of a Christmas tree and bit the star off the top.

"Delicious," he told the little girl. "Thank you, angel."

"Great family event," Cal said, taking a cookie in the shape of a bell.

"The kids are enjoying themselves," Sam added.

Cal nodded. "The new Santa House adds a nice touch to the village square this year," boasted the proud mayor, gesturing at all the people standing in line to visit Santa.

Sam nodded to the leggy blonde in a tight red sweater and skimpy red skirt with white fur trim who was hovering close to Santa. "I think Mrs. Claus is adding the best touch."

The two of them laughed, and it felt good to relax and just enjoy the night. Later, after Cal left to join the crowd at the gingerbread tent, Sam's attention turned back toward Melanie, standing in line with her son waiting to see Santa. Right now, she was smiling, but the tightness at the corners of her mouth indicated to him that she was trying too hard. Only when she was talking to her son did she seem truly happy.

Doug Stanley, the owner of the Pine Tree Motel where Sam had booked a room, had told him that Melanie was beginning to receive national attention for her antique car restoration business and was "no slouch" as a mechanic, either. Doug said she could tell what was wrong with a car just by listening to it run. And if it wasn't running, she could tell you why not in five minutes flat.

Now that was talent, and very rare in a woman, but Sam could already see that she was no ordinary woman, and a great mother, too.

Little Kyle was lucky to grow up in a place like this. A place where his grandfather stood nearby, eyes shimmering with love for his grandson. A place where a little boy could hear his mother laugh as he lobbed snowballs at her.

Maybe it would make up for the fact that Kyle didn't have a father.

A familiar heaviness tightened Sam's chest. It was his fault that Kyle didn't have a father.

Sam moved closer to Santa's House when he noticed that Kyle was next in line and couldn't help overhear his conversation.

"Ho, ho, ho," Santa said. "What's your name, young man?"

"Kyle. Kyle Bennett." The child threw a leg over Santa's and pulled himself into the big man's lap.

He looked so small and innocent, and Sam was glad that Kyle still believed in Santa Claus and the magic of Christmas.

"And what would you like for Christmas, Kyle?" Santa asked.

"I want my daddy back."

A sudden hush descended over the crowd. Santa didn't move, but Melanie took her son's hand and held it. Everyone waited to see what would happen next.

Kyle's words were a sucker punch to Sam's gut. He couldn't take in enough air, could barely think.

The boy pulled on the fur trim of Santa's collar. "Santa? Did you hear me?"

Santa glanced at Melanie.

"That's not possible, sweetie." Melanie cupped Kyle's cheek. "We talked about this before. Daddy is in heaven and—"

"I know, but I want him to come back."

"But you know that can't be," Melanie said softly. "Won't you tell Santa what *toy* you'd like for Christmas?"

Santa rubbed Kyle's back. "Santa knows that your father is in heaven watching out for you. He can see what a fine boy you are."

Kyle frowned and shook his head.

"I want him down here, not up there."

"Your daddy knows how much you like to play hockey. Would you like Santa to bring you a new hockey stick?" Santa asked hopefully.

"Okay," Kyle said quietly, shrugging his shoulders.

Sam sighed. He'd rather be anywhere except here, listening to a little boy asking Santa to bring his father back. He'd hoped this trip would resolve some issues, restore his confidence so he could do his job. Instead, he now had two more faces he'd never be able to forget.

"What's your favorite hockey team, Kyle?" Santa asked. "The Ducks?"

"The Ducks are weenies. I like the Canucks."

Sam laughed. He couldn't help himself. The

boy's innocent honesty was unexpected and a welcome relief from the serious mood.

Melanie whirled toward him, her eyes narrowed. She left Kyle with Santa and grabbed Sam by the arm, pulling him away from the crowd.

"Mr. LeDoux, I'm glad you think this is all so funny."

He could see fire in Melanie's emerald eyes by the glow of the Christmas lights on the trees overhead. Snowflakes clung to her eyelashes and her gold-blond hair. He liked this protective side of her.

"Mrs. Bennett, you misunderstand," he said softly, wishing he could brush the snow from her hair. "I'm Canadian, and I used to play for the Canucks."

She looked startled, and he thought a blush touched her cheeks. Looking down, she must have seen that her hand was still on his arm. She snatched it away, and he missed that simple contact between them.

"Melanie," he began, but she interrupted him.

"Forgiveness. That's what you want, isn't it?"

He blinked in surprise. She was right. He wanted forgiveness. Peace of mind. Absolution. Whatever she wanted to call it.

"I'm not sure that I can give you what you want. I'm just not ready." She looked into his eyes, and he thought he saw a glint of regret. "I'm sorry."

He nodded. "I'll wait."

"I don't know when—"

"I'll be in town for a while, doing whatever it is a grand marshal does. When you want to talk, give me a yell. I'll be the one with the crown and scepter."

He could have sworn a slight smile touched Melanie's lips before she walked away.

Chapter Three

The next day, Melanie reached for the rag in the pocket of her coveralls and wiped a damaged piece of the doorjamb on a four-door, 1929 Franklin dual-cowl Phaeton. Studying the damaged car part, she knew that it was made from wood and not metal. It was commonly made from ash, and she knew she'd have to cut a new one herself. Luckily, she had just the right board in the storage room.

She'd been working on the Phaeton for a collector for the past eight months. It was one of about five or six left in the world, and she was trying to talk him into donating the vehicle to a museum. She believed that everyone should have a chance to appreciate a classic car like the Phaeton.

It was good to think about her work, rather than the turmoil of her life.

She rubbed her hands together to warm them in the cold garage. Although the four industrial heaters hanging from each corner of the ceiling were turned on high, it wasn't enough to penetrate through all the layers of clothing she wore to warm her bones. Her fingers were like icicles.

Glancing out the window in the big doors of the bay, she saw it was snowing outside—big, fluffy flakes. The picture-perfect snow was a reminder of the picture-perfect Christmas she wanted to give Kyle.

Tonight, someone else would again dress as Santa and read *The Grinch Who Stole Christmas* at the public library. Tomorrow, there'd be a snowman-making contest back at the town square. After that, a peewee hockey game at Tucker's Pond, complete with bonfire, then a free skate and a craft sale. Events were scheduled for nearly every day throughout the next three weeks, and she and Kyle would be attending or participating in all of them.

Soon, she and Kyle would cut their own tree and bring it home and decorate it. They'd go caroling with the church choir and do some Christmas shopping together. They might be small steps to take, but they were important to her—and hopefully special for Kyle. In the meantime, though, it was business as usual.

As she removed the rest of the doorjamb from the car, Melanie heard voices in the office. She assumed it was her father coming in to have some coffee and talk. Since his "retirement" from Hawk's Garage, he hadn't missed a day. Jack was probably with him, anxious to get to work on one of his race cars. Then again, maybe it was Brian, ready to work on one of his endless spreadsheets or to hunt down some parts for her on the Internet.

She looked at the office and saw her father and her two brothers waving and grinning from behind the floor-to-ceiling glass wall that separated the office from the garage.

Coffee and doughnuts, a little gossip with whoever stopped in, then work. That was the usual routine at Hawk's Garage, built on the site of Ezra Packard Hawkins's smithy. In time, Ezra's sons had turned it into a carriage-repair business and called it Hawkins Livery. With the invention of the automobile, the business was renamed Hawk's Garage and transformed into a gas station and auto-repair business.

Melanie's father had added another wing to the garage for classic car restoration and their race-car division. Jack kept the division purposely small, preferring to be very selective in the projects he undertook. Melanie had taken a shine to the intricacies of making antique cars new again, although she still liked to keep her mechanical skills up-to-date in the main repairs and maintenance garage when she had the time.

Brian was less mechanically inclined. Armed with his MBA, he handled the business end and was in charge of finances. Their dad freelanced whenever the spirit moved him.

Melanie always felt secure and loved just knowing that her family was around her. They were her strength, her lifeline. Sure, they worried about her too much and they were overprotective, but she loved them for their support and caring, especially after Mike died.

Melanie sighed. Since last night, she couldn't stop thinking about Sam LeDoux. Her entire family liked him—and so did everyone else in Hawk's Lake. What did they know that she didn't? Was she wrong not to hear him out?

Maybe that would make *him* feel better, but not her.

She'd always tried to keep her pain to herself. As a kid, she hadn't had any girlfriends—they couldn't understand why she'd rather rebuild an engine than chase boys. Her brothers were always hell-bent on teasing her, so they'd be the last two on earth she'd ever confide in. Nor could she talk to her mom, who'd had health issues, and her father had enough worries between her mother being sick and the garage.

So little by little, she'd built a wall around herself—a wall that had become thicker and taller since her marriage.

Lately, she was starting to see the defects in that wall, hairline cracks that continued to grow until it was threatening to fall down around her, leaving her defenses exposed for what they were—lies, half-truths and face-saving devices.

The real truth was that Melanie was afraid of what she might see if she looked inside herself—and too deep into her marriage. There was an empty void in her mind the night of the ice storm. She knew something had happened that night that she couldn't—or didn't want to—remember.

Melanie sighed. It'd be so much easier to continue to blame Sam LeDoux than to try and see through the gauzy recesses of her mind.

Tossing and turning all night, she'd thought about the tree lighting and how she'd reacted when she'd found out who he was. She'd be-

come a different woman from the one who had
nearly flirted with him earlier—and she didn't
like that side of herself. After all, Sam had only
wanted to explain what had happened that fateful night—and she'd shut him down.

It had been easier to dislike him when she
hadn't yet met him, and hadn't seen the pain in
his eyes, an ache so similar to her own.

Did that make her a horrible person?

She found the piece of wood she'd been
looking for and walked back into the garage.
Another noise signaled that she wasn't alone.
Instead, there was Sam LeDoux himself, leaning against the wall of the garage, wearing a
black leather bomber jacket and snug, faded
jeans. To her utter mortification, something inside her sizzled.

Why was she so aware of every little detail
about him?

"Hello, Melanie. I hope I'm not interrupting you."

She turned her attention back to the doorjamb, trying to calm the flickers in her belly
caused by his deep, sexy voice. "You are."

Ignoring her response, he asked, "How did
you become involved in fixing up antique cars?"

She shrugged. "I don't know exactly. I guess
I always liked restoring things to their original

state—especially old things. My aunt Betty got me into restoring antique furniture first, and cars came next."

Why was she telling him all this? She focused on the wood in her hands, preparing it for the jigsaw.

"I think it's wonderful that you're so successful at it." He shifted on his feet, and Melanie figured that he had run out of things to say. "Listen, could I buy you a cup of coffee when you're done?"

She moved her safety goggles into place and flipped the switch on the jig. It roared to life. Sam stood with his hands in his jacket, awaiting her answer. Couldn't he take a hint?

"I already had coffee," she finally said over the noise of the saw.

"Okay. Then how about dinner tonight?"

He couldn't possibly be asking me out, she thought.

She shut off the jig and studied her cut. Perfect. "As you can see, I'm busy."

"What about the tomorrow night?"

"Busy."

To avoid looking at him, Melanie walked down to the other side of the car and inspected the grill. She already knew there was nothing wrong with it, but she measured it just for something to do.

As Sam walked toward her, Melanie felt heat rising in her blood. She told herself that it was anger, nothing more. It certainly wasn't because he was so handsome and she could smell his outdoorsy scent. His friendly smile made her think of his sensuous lips.

Darn it. What was wrong with her?

The sound of his saddle-colored cowboy boots came even closer as he walked across the concrete floor. Unable to help herself, she looked up and saw that his black hair was wind-blown and damp from the snow.

A telltale blush crept up her neck and settled on her cheeks.

She waited until her father and brother were bent over the engine of Jack's race car and out of hearing range before she spoke. "What do you want, Sam?"

In the overhead lights, his eyes were like the color of Hawk's Lake in the summer.

"To talk."

Melanie could feel him standing behind her, so she went back around to the other side of the car to get away from him.

He huffed out a breath, clearly frustrated by her refusal. "Look, I spoke with Cal. Since my presence is clearly making things uncomfortable for you, I tried to get out of being the grand marshal, but he said that they couldn't get a replacement at this point." He shrugged. "I just want you to know that I tried."

Melanie froze. He'd actually tried to get out of being the grand marshal—for *her*? That was considerate of him. Maybe she *was* being too selfish.

Emotions were churning inside her, giving her a pounding headache. A nagging voice inside her chastised her for being unfair. Maybe listening to him would help her put the past to rest and make it easier for her to have a good Christmas with Kyle.

She sighed. "Okay, Sam… I'll have dinner with you. Tomorrow night."

He smiled. "Shall I pick you up? Seven o'clock?"

She shook her head. "I'll meet you at Momma Luigi's. It's on Main Street."

"I'll find it," he said. "It's a date."

"No, it's not," she said, ignoring the flush of pleasure that heated her face. "It's just dinner."

Sam found himself whistling as he drove back to the Pine Tree Motel in Jack Hawkins's big white pickup, which he'd borrowed for the length of his stay.

He liked both Melanie's brothers, and her father, too. He'd gotten to know them fairly well last year after the ice storm. They were hard workers, friendly and personable.

But he was attracted to Melanie—he couldn't deny it. In fact, it was one of the reasons he agreed to return to Hawk's Lake.

What had made Melanie decide to have dinner with him? Sam figured he'd just worn her down and she was sick of him asking. He could be tenacious when he wanted to be—really tenacious.

She looked sexy in her navy blue mechanic's jumpsuit. It clung to all her curves. Her emerald eyes looked even bigger and greener through the safety goggles she was wearing.

And she'd *finally* agreed to hear him out— and for the first time in months, he felt a lightness inside his chest.

Later that evening, the snow was still falling in big feathery flakes as Melanie pulled her forest-green Blazer into the parking lot across the street from the Hawk's Lake Public Library.

She smiled down at her son. "We're here."

"Cool," Kyle said, grinning. "I can't wait to talk to Santa."

"Santa's only reading *The Grinch* today. You already talked to Santa last night." She got out and opened the passenger door for Kyle, who quickly scrambled out of the Blazer.

"Hold it, mister," she said. "It's twenty degrees out."

She pulled his hat down around his ears, gathered the hood of his parka onto his head and snapped it under his chin. With his sweet face framed in a circle, he looked like a little angel. She took his mittened hand in hers and walked to the street to wait for one of the town's four snowplows to go by.

Pretty soon Kyle wouldn't believe in Santa or the magic of Christmas. Soon he'd be too grown-up to take her hand to cross the street. She sighed. Funny, she thought, how time could be a friend or an enemy.

As they were about to cross, a big white pickup truck ground to a slow, sputtering halt before them. It was driven by... Santa Claus.

Kyle squealed. "It's Santa, Mom! It's Santa! What's he doing in Uncle Jack's truck?"

Santa got out of the truck, and it looked like he was about to let loose with an expletive before he saw them standing there. Familiar blue eyes met hers above the white beard.

Santa shifted on his feet, looking down. "Um...ho, ho, ho!" he said weakly. "Um... my reindeer are resting and my sleigh is being loaded by my elves, so a nice man by the name of Jack Hawkins let me use his...uh...sleigh on wheels. But there seems to be something wrong with it."

Melanie knew that voice. That deep, resonating voice. It seemed to melt her bones every time she heard it.

Sam LeDoux.

"Santa, my mom can fix it," Kyle said, eyes wide, looking up at the big man. "My grandpa says she's the best car fixer in the whole world." He swiveled to look at her. "You can fix it, right, Mom?"

"Um...yes...of course, I'll take a look under the hood, honey." She walked Kyle to a nearby bench and brushed the snow from it. "You sit right there and don't move. There are a lot of cars driving into the library lot and it's dark. This'll only take a second."

"Okay." Kyle watched her with excitement glowing on his face, like his mom helping Santa Claus was the best thing that had ever happened.

Walking back to the truck, she flipped the lever and bent over to look under the hood as Santa—Sam—stood next to her. Their shoulders brushed as they stood side by side looking at the engine.

"Why are *you* playing Santa?" she said through gritted teeth.

He looked down at her and grinned. "The scheduled Santa had to work overtime at the paper mill, so I got roped into it by Cal."

"I see."

Two days in Hawk's Lake and Sam had been roped into playing Santa. By his own admission, he had at least a dozen bigger events to attend, yet he'd come for the kids. She had to admit he wasn't quite the bad guy she'd made him out to be...

"I'm not sure that I'll be a very good Santa," Sam said, shaking his head. "Any advice for a rookie?"

As she looked up into those twinkling eyes, she had to laugh. "Just be natural and do a lot of ho-ho-ho-ing. And by the way, Jack's truck needs a new alternator."

"You can tell that right off?" He sounded impressed.

"I could tell by the sound when you pulled in," she said confidently. "I'll call my cousin

Ronnie at the garage to send a tow." She shook her head. "I don't know why Jack loaned you this truck. He knew the alternator was going. Ronnie will fix it tonight."

She closed the hood, then turned a critical eye to Sam's outfit.

"Sam, your beard and your…stomach…are a bit off center. You should fix them."

"I've tried, but I can't seem to get them straight."

It was dark behind the truck, and he was standing much too close to her, but Melanie couldn't let the kids see Sam in his disheveled state.

She hurriedly moved his beard to the left, so the mustache was positioned correctly around his lips—his *perfect* lips. Glancing down to his stomach, she centered the pillows in the middle of his body.

She could smell peppermint on his breath and pine-scented cologne. His eyes were no longer full of amusement, but seemed to watch her with a very different kind of intensity.

"There," she said, embarrassed by her husky voice. "Much better."

"Thank you," he said, but he didn't back up. She couldn't stop looking at his eyes, glittering in the moonlight. What secrets were hidden behind those blue depths?

She shook her head and reminded herself that she didn't want to know him well enough to find out.

Melanie stepped back, found her cell phone in her purse, motioned for Kyle to join them, and called cousin Ronnie at the garage. She put in the order for a tow while Sam got a red sack out of the front seat of the truck.

"Santa's reading *How the Grinch Stole Christmas*," Sam said to Kyle in his Santa voice. He looked at Melanie and cleared his throat. "Ho, ho, ho."

"I know," Kyle said, looking up in awe. "It's my favorite."

Melanie listened to the snow crunching under their boots. She'd rather be digging a tunnel through a glacier with a spoon than be in the same room with Sam LeDoux. He made her feel things she didn't want to feel—but she couldn't disappoint her son.

"I'll show you the way, Santa," Kyle said.

"Ho, ho, ho! That's a good boy."

Kyle seemed to be growing taller as he led Sam into the library. The children squealed in glee when they saw Santa, and Sam eventually relaxed and played the part enthusiastically.

Melanie took a chair at the side of the room while he motioned for the children to gather around him on the floor. Then he read *The Grinch* to the packed room of kids, parents and library staff.

He seemed like he was having the time of his life, Melanie thought. Every kid stared up at him mesmerized. His deep, resonant voice echoed through the hushed library, and his Grinch voice was sufficiently creepy.

The children stared up at him, caught up in the fantasy of Christmas in the happy hamlet of Whoville.

Melanie watched as a tiny girl inched closer and closer until she was touching Sam's knee. He absentmindedly pulled her into his lap, tucking her halo of dark curls into the crook of one arm. She looked up at him, transfixed by every word.

Melanie was transfixed, too. Could a man who played Santa so naturally be all that bad?

The story ended and Santa received a round of applause and cheers. He motioned to Kyle to come forward. "Kyle, would you like to help Santa pass out candy canes?"

Kyle nodded so enthusiastically she thought he was going to fall over. With pride, Melanie watched as her son carefully handed each person a candy cane and politely answered, "You're welcome" to every "Thank you."

The library emptied out, except for one mother and a little towheaded girl. The girl stood next to Kyle watching the fish swim in an aquarium in the corner of the room.

Melanie heard the woman tell Sam that they were staying nearby at the Mountain Lake Lodge on Blue Lake. She explained that they were rebuilding their home after an electrical fire, but construction was moving slowly due to the snow and frozen ground.

"Would you mind if my daughter, Emily, talked to you for a minute?" she asked Sam, hope etched into her face. "She's still upset about the fire."

Melanie's heart squeezed as Sam said, "Of course."

The woman went to get Emily. The girl seemed painfully shy, barely looking at Santa. She clutched the hem of her mother's jacket in a death grip. But when Sam patted his knee, the girl scrambled up into his lap. So much for her shyness.

"And what is your name?"

"Emily Farley. I'm seven years old."

"Have you been a good girl, Emily?"

Emily's eyes grew wide, and she looked to

her mother for affirmation. Her mother nodded. "Yes."

Sam took her hand and held it. "Santa knows that you had a fire at your house. That must have scared you."

Tears glistened in Emily's eyes as she nodded, and Melanie's heart ached for the little girl.

He patted her head. "Santa knows you were very brave," Sam said gently. "Your house will be ready soon. And it'll be nice and special and all new just for you." Sam held up a tissue. "Close your eyes."

Emily closed her eyes, and Sam blotted them carefully with a tissue. "Now smile for Santa."

The child's grin lit up like lights on a tree.

Melanie smiled. Sam had handled the situation perfectly. Melanie warmed up to him a little more.

Sam smoothed back the little girl's hair. "Emily, since you've been such a good girl, what would you like for Christmas?"

"A Katie Ann doll and the Katie Ann town house. And some clothes for Katie Ann. And Katie Ann's boat and trailer, too."

Emily's mother took her little hand. "Sweetheart, I'm sure Santa will do what he can." As her words faded she looked away, wiping her eyes.

Sam held the little girl's chin in a gloved

hand. "Santa always tries to make Christmas wishes come true. Now, why don't you ask Kyle to give you another candy cane."

Emily's mother shook her head and sniffed. It was obvious that she couldn't afford all those toys.

Sam took her arm and moved her away from Kyle and Emily, who were peeling candy canes and chattering like long-lost pals.

"Mrs. Farley." Sam handed her a tissue and winked. "There's no crying on Grinch night."

The woman chuckled and wiped her eyes. "It's just…it's been so hard since the fire, and I want to give Emily an especially nice Christmas."

Melanie's stomach churned. She knew exactly how Mrs. Farley felt.

"Have faith, Mrs. Farley," Sam said. "As I told Emily, Santa always tries to make Christmas wishes come true. That means yours, too."

Mrs. Farley was smiling as she turned and walked over to Emily. Sam LeDoux had put that smile on her face with his encouraging words.

Melanie wiped at her own eyes with the tail of her red wool scarf, horrified when he looked her way.

He gave her a wink and a smile, and she

found herself smiling back, lost once more in his twinkling blue eyes.

When was she going to come to her senses and realize that Sam LeDoux wasn't really Santa Claus? There was no way he could make things better for her. There were no magic words he could say, nothing he could do to bring Kyle's father back.

Sure, she was starting to like some things about him, but what did that matter? Her "best Christmas ever" plan didn't include Sam LeDoux. She needed to focus on that goal and not let him distract her.

Sam looked at her with a smile that made her heart race—a smile that was far too sexy for Santa Claus. And Melanie knew that, for better or worse, she was already distracted.

Chapter Four

"Melanie, would you mind giving me a lift to Hawk's Garage?" Sam asked. "Maybe my sleigh on wheels is repaired."

Before she could reply, Kyle answered for her. "Sure, Santa!"

As soon as they climbed into the car Melanie knew it was a mistake to put Sam in the front seat next to her. He was too close, intruding on her senses.

Kyle took no notice of her discomfort. He was giddy that Santa was riding in his mother's car and kept up a steady stream of chatter about everything and anything. Sam laughed a lot, staying in character all the while. He was clearly enjoying Kyle's excitement.

Melanie let herself relax a bit, as much as she could with Sam so close. The low timbre of his voice was masculine and every so often she'd catch a unique pronunciation of a word—traces of his French accent coming through. The white beard around his face contrasted with his tanned skin. Maybe his latest disaster had taken him to a tropical island.

Preoccupied by her evaluations, she almost ran a stop sign.

She hit her brakes and they skidded on the snow-covered mountain road. "Oops."

"Careful—it's slick out here," Sam said.

Her heart beat wildly. She assumed that it was due to the close call on the icy road instead of Sam's sexy accent.

"Why do you talk that way, Santa Claus?" Kyle asked.

"You mean my accent? It's French. You see, Kyle, Santa knows other languages, like French, because he travels all over the world."

Nice recovery. Sam could sure think on his feet.

"Hey, Santa, will you say something in French?" Kyle asked.

"*Joyeux Noël.* That means Merry Christmas."

"Noo-ell." Kyle giggled.

Melanie had to smile as Sam spent the next few miles teaching Kyle a couple of lines from a French Christmas carol, and in spite of Melanie's resolve to dislike anything and everything about Sam, she found herself laughing and enjoying his interaction with her son.

Finally, she made the turn into Hawk's Garage and saw her father walking out of the office. She rolled her window down.

"Hi, Dad."

"Hello, Mel."

"Hi, Grandpa!" Kyle piped up.

"How are you doing, tiger?" With a big grin, Ed pointed to the front seat. "Is that who I think it is?"

"It's Santa Claus, Grandpa!"

"Ho, ho, ho!" Sam added helpfully.

"Well, Mr. Claus, your truck is all ready," Ed said. "Ronnie is the best and the fastest with alternators."

"There will be a special present under his tree this Christmas for helping Santa," Sam said.

"Oh, cool, look at that!" Kyle hopped out of the car and took off running toward a huge snowplow that Ronnie had been repairing on the side of the garage.

Heaven only knew what went on in a boy's mind, but it appeared that even Santa took a backseat where heavy equipment was concerned.

Melanie took the key from the pegboard and handed it to Sam. Her mouth went dry as his hand closed over hers. She waited for him to release it, but he didn't.

"Thank you for the speedy service. What do I owe you?"

That was a loaded question.

"Nothing, of course. It's Jack's truck." She should have removed her hand, but she was enjoying the warmth that flooded her body.

"Then I'll see you tomorrow evening at Momma Luigi's," he said.

"I'll be there."

He let go of her hand, and she felt cold again.

Sam stared into the flickering light of a red candle stuck into a straw-covered Chianti bottle, absentmindedly chipping off the wax that had dripped along the bottle's side.

As he waited for Melanie, he wondered for the hundredth time if he was doing the right thing by talking to her, or if he'd only make things worse. How could he make things worse?

He simply wanted to explain his side of what had happened that fateful night.

Do you want me to forgive you?

Her questions had echoed in his head as he tried to sleep last night. So had the answer: yes. That's exactly what he wanted. But he also wanted to make sure that Melanie and Kyle were managing okay, but he wasn't quite satisfied that they were. And he wanted to apologize for what had happened.

He glanced in the direction of the door and saw Melanie walk in, looking like she'd rather be anywhere else. Putting down his glass of beer, he stood and watched as she approached. She looked terrific in black pants and a forest-green ski jacket that set off her golden-blond hair. When she glanced in his direction, he waved. She nodded and began to weave through the tables, acknowledging acquaintances with a cheerful smile, which dimmed as she came closer to him.

"Hello, Melanie." He extended his hand, and she shook it. Despite the cold, her hand was warm, and so small in his. For a woman who worked in a garage, she had the softest skin, and just for a moment he imagined her touching him...

Suddenly realizing that he was just standing

and staring, waiting for heaven knows what, he pulled out her chair.

"Thank you," she said as she sat down and picked up a menu, clearly determined to maintain some distance.

"How about a truce? At least for dinner."

She sighed. "All right."

"Great." He smiled, feeling a bit better. "We're making progress already."

"Of course, we could always hurry and eat and then get back to normal," she said.

They both laughed.

"Who's watching Kyle?"

"Brian. They're going to the high-school auditorium to see *Miracle on 34th Street.* It's another Snow Festival event. There's popcorn and hot cocoa and a sing-a-long after the movie."

"Oh, that's right. It was on my schedule, but the grand marshal wasn't needed." He grinned. "What a great idea for the kids. Kyle will like that."

Taking a sip of beer, he watched how the flickering candlelight brought out different shades of gold in her hair and the depth of her green eyes. If only she'd focus that incredible gaze on him and see him as a man, and not associate him with her husband... But that wasn't likely to happen.

Suddenly, he wanted to help her revise her opinion of him. Badly.

As Melanie continued to read the menu, the silence between them seemed more comfortable. He was having a hard time sitting still, and his hand itched to take hers.

Normally, he'd question his sanity, but he knew exactly what was wrong with him—he was attracted to Melanie Bennett. And he suspected that deep down she felt the same way about him, and hated herself for it.

Guilt and regret washed over him. Both had been his constant companions for almost a year. He'd tried drinking his thoughts away, but that hadn't helped. It had only left him more depressed when the numbness wore off. He'd tried throwing himself into his job, but he questioned everything he did, every decision he made. Finally, he'd decided not to be a manager, but a volunteer instead.

He decided to be upfront with her.

"Melanie…"

She looked up from her menu.

"Not a day goes by that I don't think about that night. I want to tell you that I am so sorry," he said quietly, meeting her gaze.

Her eyes grew wide as she stared at him. "I told myself that this would be a mistake."

She shook her head. "This is too awkward. Too hard."

"If it's any consolation, it's not any easier for me."

"Then why are we having this conversation?" She gritted her teeth. "Let's just leave it alone."

"Please hear me out."

Was it the emotion in his voice? His hope? He didn't know, but a rush of relief washed through him when she leaned back as if she'd decided to listen.

"Look, I know you want to talk about it," she said, her eyes on the place setting instead of on him. "But I just can't."

"I wanted to talk to you after the storm, but you were recovering from a concussion, and I was advised not to." He stopped talking when he saw the confusion and pain on her face.

"Sam, some things are just better left unsaid, better left contained. Did you ever hear the myth of Pandora's box? I don't want to open up the box. I'm afraid of what might get out."

"If I remember the story correctly," he said gently, "Pandora did open the box, and unleashed some bad stuff, but she managed to save hope."

She looked at him with such a sad expression he thought his heart would break.

Melanie took a deep breath. "I know I said I didn't want to discuss the ice storm, but there's one thing that I want to ask you, Sam."

"You can ask me anything."

"Why didn't you attend Mike's funeral?" She put the menu down on the table and met his eyes.

"After I got out of the hospital—"

"You were in the hospital?" Melanie's brows rose. "Why?"

"Hypothermia. And frostbite. After I jumped into the water to pull Mike out, the doctors were watching a couple of toes."

"So you tried to save Mike." It was more of a question than a statement. Her luscious lips came together in a thin line, and she wasn't even blinking. "Were you okay?"

"Yes—they let me go after a couple of days." Sam sat back in his chair, confused, then angry. No one had told her anything during the past year? "Did you think that I abandoned him?"

"Like you said, I had a concussion. No one talked much about the details." She rubbed her head as if she was getting a headache, but he couldn't stop now.

They sure left out a big detail, Sam thought.

"I'd sent him to cut branches off a tree— they'd gotten tangled in the power lines. The tree fell into the river." Sam bit his lip. "It was so dark, and I couldn't find him at first. When I finally spotted him, I tried to get him above water, to pull him out, but it was hopeless. The water was icy and the current was moving so fast and with the snow... I was able to get us to the bank where your brothers helped us out. Anyway, I just want you to know that I tried my best."

"Excuse me."

He looked up as Melanie's chair scraped against the floor, and then she was gone.

He sat there alone, thinking back to the mistakes he'd made that night. How he should have seen that Mike Bennett was in no condition to work. He'd smelled alcohol on his breath, but there was no way to know if Mike had had one drink or ten. Sam should have known better than to send him up that wrecked tree, but Mike had insisted that he could do it. Everyone else had been busy and they were all working against the clock to get the power restored.

Against his better judgment, he hadn't sent Mike home.

He'd sent him to his death.

Chapter Five

Melanie leaned against the sink in the ladies' room, splashed cold water on her face to calm herself, then took a long, hard look in the mirror. Her makeup was dripping down her face, water drops stained her blouse, and she was feeling the start of a headache.

After the accident, she'd refused to read the articles in the papers about the ice storm. Between her concussion and the shock of losing Mike, she didn't remember much. Nor did she want to remember. Her father and brothers barely talked about the incident in front of her—doctor's orders, they'd told her. Her father par-

celed out information only when she asked, and
she rarely had.

Melanie just assumed that everyone called
Sam LeDoux a hero because he'd helped the
town recover from the ice storm. She'd never
realized that he'd jumped into the icy, raging
river to save her husband.

A shadow of a memory, an image of Mike
returning from a trip that fateful night, crept
into the shadowy corners of her mind. Then
came the sick feeling of guilt.

She'd always had a problem with guilt. When
she was in high school and other kids her age
snuck out at night for bonfires down at the lake,
she'd joined them a couple of times. But it was
never fun for her. She knew that her parents
would be worried if they found her missing,
and she couldn't do that to them.

But one humid summer night, she'd snuck
out to meet Mike, and got pregnant with Kyle.

How his parents, wealthy business people
from Palm Beach, hated the thought of their son
marrying a woman from little Hawk's Lake,
and a mechanic to boot. They had accused her
of trapping him, refused to attend the wedding
and wouldn't even listen to her when she de-
nied their accusations.

Subsequently, with Mike gone most of the

time on his football scouting trips, Melanie had thrown herself into raising Kyle and building her antique car restoration business. And over the past year, she'd used the little energy she had left blaming Sam LeDoux.

What else didn't she know? What else couldn't she remember? She covered her face with her hands. What was wrong with her?

"Are you okay, Melanie?"

She jumped, shocked by the intrusion. Mavis Braddock, the owner of the Pine and Holly Gift Shop on Main Street, put a hand on her arm. She was a tall, thin woman with bright white hair who always looked worried no matter what the occasion. Mavis handed her a plastic bag containing folded blue tissues.

Melanie took it. "Thanks, Mavis."

"Are you ill, dear?"

"I think I'm getting a cold." Melanie blew her nose, then took more tissues and blotted her face.

"It's the season," Mavis said. "I saw you sitting with that handsome Sam LeDoux. He seems like such a nice young man."

Melanie pinched the bridge of her nose, wondering when her headache was going to stop. "Yes. He is." She managed a smile and handed back the bag of tissues. "Thanks. You're very kind."

As Mavis went into one of the stalls, Melanie took another look in the mirror and knew what she had to do.

She was going to have to calm down, rein in her emotions, and bide her time until Sam left Hawk's Lake. He'd apologized, told her his side of the story. Surely he could let it go now. But she sensed that he was the type of man who did everything with a purpose—and that he wasn't finished yet.

Sam stood as Melanie returned from the ladies' room, and held her chair out for her.

"Are you all right?" he asked.

"Fine."

A slight twist of his mouth told her that he didn't believe her. "Look, I'm sorry I upset you. Let's not talk about the storm anymore. Please, relax and try to enjoy dinner."

The blue depths of his eyes were so sincere. Why did he have to have such nice eyes? And why did his hair look so soft?

And *why* was she noticing all these things about him?

Thankfully, Concetta Luigi appeared at their table to take their order. "Hello, Melanie. Ready to order?" She was so engrossed in staring at Sam that she barely glanced Melanie's way.

"Fine, Chickie," Melanie said, using the woman's high-school nickname. "This is Sam LeDoux." She gestured toward Sam.

"Hell-o, Sam." She sung his name, making the one syllable go on forever. "You look more handsome in person than in the papers."

Sam grinned. "Thank you, uh… Chickie."

"I'd like veal parmigiana and a small salad," Melanie said.

"Got it, Mel." Chickie scribbled on a pad, still not taking her eyes off Sam. "How about you, sweetheart?" She smiled like a woman with a secret. "Do you see anything you like?"

The double meaning obviously wasn't lost on Sam. His eyes twinkled in amusement, and Melanie felt a little tweak of inadequacy. She'd never learned how to flirt, not that she would ever want to be so obvious, so transparent.

So why was Chickie irritating her?

Chickie leaned over Sam LeDoux and pointed to a column on the menu. "Here are our specials." An ample breast settled on his bicep.

Eventually, Sam cleared his throat, moved his arm and handed her the menu. "I'll have the same as Melanie. And another beer, please."

"Iced tea for me," added Melanie.

"I'll be right back," Chickie winked at Sam, and he smiled in return. As she sashayed away, he turned his attention back to Melanie.

"She's divorced and obviously looking," Melanie volunteered.

"Not interested," Sam said, draining what was left of his beer.

"Then you're married?" She was just making conversation; she knew he wasn't married. For some reason, her father had pounced on the fact right away and made it known to her.

His turquoise-blue eyes studied her. "I've never been married. I travel too much to settle down. The few serious relationships that I've had never lasted. People don't like to be left constantly."

"I know the feeling."

Chickie delivered the salads, a basket of Italian bread and their drinks. Melanie noticed that her white blouse was unbuttoned another notch. When she bent over, she practically tossed her breasts in Sam's face. To his credit, he ignored her efforts.

Sam chuckled when she left. "You're right. She's pretty obvious."

They both laughed and that seemed to clear the air between them.

They ate in silence for a while, and all Melanie could think about was that she might have done him an injustice.

She took a deep breath. "Sam, thank you for trying to save Mike," she said, afraid that her voice would tremble. "Mike and I—well, we'd been having some problems, which just makes everything harder to deal with."

Sam waved a hand in dismissal. "Anyone would have done the same thing."

"But they didn't. You did."

He shook his head. "Let's not talk about it."

Their eyes locked, and Melanie saw hope and something more in Sam's eyes, something that sent a warm flutter up her spine, something that made her anxious and nervous and…excited.

"Maybe you'll meet someone special again, Melanie," Sam said.

"No," she said softly. "I won't let myself get hurt like that ever again."

Before Sam could ask another question, their dinners arrived. And while Melanie found herself enjoying Sam's company, she couldn't help wondering why the man she'd sworn to stay away from was getting under her skin.

And why she was minding less and less.

After dinner, they stood in front of Momma Luigi's as a light snow fell. It glittered as it drifted to earth, sparkling in the glow of the moon and swirling in the beam of the lights around the parking lot.

"Let me walk you to your car," he said. "It's a bit icy in the parking lot."

"I'm used to it. And you should be, too, living in Canada."

He nodded. "We got a ton of snow every year when I lived in Lenore, which is a lot like Hawk's Lake. The elevation's not as high, but there's lake effect snow from Lake Ontario."

She took the arm he offered and began walking to the parking lot on the right side of the building. "Lenore. I like the name."

"Lenore was my great-great-great grandmother. Her husband, Jacques, adored her and decided that she needed a village named after her."

"Just like my old ancestor, Ezra Packard Hawkins. Only he named the village after himself."

"Nothing like little villages." He started to reach for her hand, but then lowered his arm. "I hope it wasn't too difficult having dinner with a man that you hate."

She took a deep breath. "That sounds so harsh."

He shrugged. "Can you deny it?"

He stood looking down at her, his blue eyes so piercing, as if he were looking deep inside her. Did he see a woman who didn't want to remember that night? A woman who blamed him for everything?

"I don't hate you anymore, Sam, and I'm glad you convinced me to go to dinner. I'm a little stubborn," she said.

He laughed. "No one's more stubborn than yours truly."

They crunched over the icy ground, finally making it to her green SUV.

"Well, this is my car," she said. "Thank you."

He nodded. "Good night, Melanie. See you around." He smiled, then turned and started walking toward the highway.

Where on earth was he going? "Wait, Sam. Where's your truck? I mean, Jack's truck?"

"Back at the Pine Tree Motel. I walked here."

"But it's dark, and when vehicles come around the bend, they can't see pedestrians."

"Melanie, you'd better be careful." A smile teased his lips. "You're almost sounding like you care."

She blushed, grateful that it was too dark for him to see. "Oh, for heaven's sake, get in my car."

"I'm fine. Really." He turned back toward the highway.

With a curse under her breath, she got into her Blazer. Soon she pulled up alongside him. "Get in. If you turn up as roadkill after our dinner, there won't be a grand marshal and the whole town will blame me."

Chuckling, Sam climbed into her car. She could feel the coldness of the night on him, yet he somehow radiated warmth and comfort.

Being this close to Sam was too intimate, maybe because this time Kyle wasn't in the backseat. And she knew more about the kind of man he was—the kind that would risk his life for a man he barely knew. The kind who awakened long-lost feelings deep inside her…

She forced herself to concentrate on the winding mountain road.

They drove the short distance in silence until Melanie pulled up in front of the Pine Tree Motel.

"Thanks for the ride," Sam said.

"You're welcome."

"See you around," he said. "I have to check my schedule, but isn't there a snowman-making contest in the morning?"

She nodded. "One of Kyle's favorite events. But I can't believe that you would want to go."

"Grand marshal, remember? It'll be fun." He was about to exit the car, then turned back to her. "I almost forgot. Where's the nearest toy store around here?"

"There's one on Main Street. It's kind of small. They have locally made things. What exactly are you looking for?"

"I don't know. Popular toys. Toys for little girls."

Hmm… Melanie remembered the conversation Sam had had with Emily. She'd bet her last dollar that he was going to buy Emily her Katie Ann toys for Christmas.

She tried not to show any emotion. He obviously wanted it to remain a secret. "You'd have to drive to Utica or Albany for that kind of thing. There's no big toy store in these mountains."

"Which is closer?" he asked.

"Utica. It's about an hour and a half drive south of here."

"Thanks. Well, I'd better get some sleep. Tomorrow's another big day for me."

"The hockey game is tomorrow, too." Why was she still making conversation? She should let him leave and get into his hotel, but darn, she suddenly didn't want the evening to end.

"That should be fun," Sam finally said. "I'm

one of the referees, along with Cal and some-one from the Glaciers."

"Kyle's playing," she said with a smile. "It's all he's been talking about for weeks. If the Polar Bears lose, there will be no living with him."

Sam raised both eyebrows and grinned. "Are you trying to influence a referee?"

The laughter bubbled up from somewhere inside her, and it felt great—and a little scary.

"No. Now get out of my car." She pushed his arm. "I have to rescue Brian from babysitting."

It took all of Melanie's willpower to insist that he leave. She enjoyed his company, enjoyed joking with him, enjoying his teasing. The tension that had been clinging to her suddenly dissolved as he closed the car door behind himself.

And—what the heck?—she couldn't wait to see him again.

Melanie Bennett had the sexiest laugh he'd ever heard, Sam decided as he unlocked the door to his room at the Pine Tree Motel.

He didn't want to be attracted to her, but he couldn't get her out of his head. Maybe it was the smile that lit up her emerald eyes. Or maybe it was because he admired how hard she was working to deal with the changes in her life.

He'd done everything he possibly could to help her during the past year, not that she would ever know. He'd referred as many clients as he could find to her. A friend of his owned the Franklin Phaeton that she was currently working on. Another friend owned the '29 Strutz roadster that was also in her workshop.

He was at a loss as to what he could do for Kyle, though.

Sam sighed. He couldn't deny the heat that ripped through him whenever he saw Melanie— or even when he thought of her. She excited him more than any woman had in a long time. But she didn't trust him, and maybe she never would. All he could do was prove to her that he was worthy of her trust, and he planned to do that—just as soon as he could figure out how.

Chapter Six

Melanie always loved the sight of the original Hawkins's homestead, situated on two acres of clearing surrounded by tall pines and shaggy Canadian hemlocks. In the spring, trillium blanketed the floor of the forest like a carpet of snow against the unfurling green ferns.

Her great-great-grandmother Helena Hawkins had named the big house Sunshine Cottage. Future occupants had kept it painted in the original shades of buttercream, gold and daffodil yellow.

Outside, deer munched on Melanie's lawn and sipped from her little pond. In the winter, she put out a salt lick for them in a fallen log in the backyard. In late spring, little fawns appeared with their mothers, balancing on wobbly legs.

Pulling the car into the driveway, she entered the mudroom through a side door. She kicked off her boots and hung up her coat and scarf in the closet.

"Kyle? Brian? Where are you guys?"

The house was too quiet. On the kitchen table, she spotted a note from her brother: "Kyle is staying with me at my house. Sleep in. We'll meet you at the snowman-making contest in the morning."

Melanie grinned at the smiley face Kyle had drawn under Brian's name. She was grateful for a night alone, especially with so much on her mind.

She thought about everything Sam had told her tonight, and knew that she could not procrastinate any longer. She had to open the box that she'd hidden in one of the cabinets in the library.

Pandora's box.

Maybe after all these months, its contents wouldn't taunt her anymore.

She made herself a cup of tea and then went into the library, one of her favorite rooms in the house. She opened the cabinet, hesitated, then pulled out the heavy box.

A month or so after Mike's funeral, she'd
made a sweep through the house and collected
all the sympathy cards that people had sent her,
along with everything else she didn't want to
look at.

Holding the box like it was a time bomb, she
walked over to the dark oak desk and sat down
on the burgundy leather chair. Turning the lamp
on, it took her another five minutes to work up
enough courage to lift the lid.

She peered inside and paused as she stared at
the jumbled contents, memories rushing back
in bits and pieces.

She pulled out a receipt for an expensive
necklace that she'd found in the pocket of Mike's
brown suede coat when she was taking it to the
cleaners. On the receipt was a typewritten message that would go on a gift card: "Happy Anniversary, Donna. My love always, Mike."

Donna McSwain had been Mike's fiancée
before Melanie became pregnant. She hadn't
known until Mike's mother informed her of
that fact when Melanie and Mike announced
they were getting married.

She pulled out a stack of receipts that were
clipped together—two year's worth for Donna's
rent. She'd found them in Mike's desk along

with a year's worth of receipts for lease payments on Donna's car.

In the corner of the box, she found two ticket stubs from *The Phantom of the Opera* in New York City. Melanie remembered checking the date against her appointment book. It was the same date as Kyle's first T-ball game, which had been preceded by a little parade of all the teams to the field.

She dipped back into the box and unfolded a receipt from a travel agent for a Caribbean cruise for two, which Mike had apparently been enjoying while Kyle was in a school play. He'd played a grandfather clock and had two lines—two lines that Mike had missed because he was vacationing with another woman. Surprise, surprise…he'd lied about being in Nebraska scouting a football player with a "pass faster than the speed of sound."

She'd confronted Mike about the cruise and everything else after he'd walked through the door that fateful night—during which he'd carried on about the kid in Nebraska.

Lies. All lies.

They had a huge fight. Thank goodness Kyle had been at Brian's.

She'd smelled the booze on his breath. It was as strong as if he'd just stopped at a bar. Then he'd been stupid enough to drive the icy, snowy mountains from the airport in Albany.

He poured himself a whiskey, chugged it down as if it were water. "I'm too tired to fight with you, Melanie."

He never drank like this before, and Melanie figured that it was giving him some liquid courage to finally face her. "How long have you been seeing Donna?"

He took another drink. "The last couple of years."

"Why? I thought we were happy."

"Maybe *you* were. But I guess I never stopped loving her. Then I decided life was too short."

She wanted to slap the drink from his hand. "If you never stopped loving Donna, why the hell did you keep hounding me to marry you?"

"I thought we could make a go of it. And I wanted my son."

"You wanted Kyle on *your* terms."

He drained his drink. "If it's any consolation, whatever I spent on Donna, I put an equal amount in an investment account for you and Kyle."

"That's decent of you," she said sarcastically.

"Listen, about the investment—"

"I don't care about the money, Mike. And

Kyle doesn't need a part-time father. I want a divorce."

He downed another three fingers of whiskey.

The siren had gone off then, its shrill whistle sounding like the scream that she wanted to let loose. There was an emergency in town.

"Saved by the bell." He slurred his words. "Or should I say the siren?" He stumbled to the door.

"You're not going anywhere. You're drunk."

"The cold air will do me good."

"You can't drive, Mike. Please, don't."

He struggled to put his coat and boots on.

"Goodbye, Melanie. I gotta answer the siren, or your father and brothers will look down their noses at me. They always have, you know. They never thought I was good enough for you." He snorted. "Can you imagine?"

"They never thought that, Mike. Never."

"Oh, yes, they did," he yelled.

He slid and stumbled down the ice-covered steps of Sunshine Cottage, but managed to stay on his feet. She remembered racing after him, yanking on his coat to get him back into the house, trying to take his keys away from him.

The wind howled, and sleet had coated her hair and turned it into ice in seconds. She didn't have any boots or a jacket on, so her teeth started to chatter immediately.

The siren wailed, and tears froze on her cheeks. She couldn't feel her hands, but she managed to grab him by the collar of his parka.

He yanked away from her, and she ran after him, then slid on the icy sidewalk.

There was blinding pain in the back of her head as it hit on the concrete. She heard a dull noise, and everything went black...

Melanie shook her head and rubbed her face. She looked around the library, trying to anchor herself in the present.

"I should have realized that he was cheating," she said to the empty room. "I should have known he was lying to me years ago."

With one swoop of her arm, she cleared the contents of the desk. The papers, reports and receipts went flying. She let out a big scream, raised her mug and threw it at the fireplace. Tea sloshed all over the room, and pieces of china scattered across the rug.

She pressed trembling hands over her eyes. She didn't know how long she sat there, but she knew she had to clean up her mess.

She made herself get up from the chair and walk over to the fireplace.

Just as she knelt down to pick up some pieces of her mug, she saw the receipt for the necklace again. It signified what a farce her marriage had been. A lie.

Finally she remembered everything. She'd blocked it all out and blamed Sam LeDoux.

And one way or another, she intended to make it up to him.

A few hours later, Sam answered the phone on his beside table. "Hello?"

"Good morning. It's Melanie. Hope I didn't wake you."

This was a surprise. "No. Just reading the paper. Lots of hot news happening in Hawk's Lake."

Melanie laughed. "Somehow I doubt that."

"What can I do for you?"

She hesitated. "Would you join me for coffee this morning? There's something I'd like to tell you."

Sam couldn't believe what he was hearing. "When?"

"How about now?"

"Sure."

"Good," she said. "Take a right out of the hotel. Follow Main Street until you come to the fire station. Make a sharp right after that onto Mountain Ledge Drive. I'm number 206."

"Got it. I'm on my way."

Twenty minutes later, Sam climbed the handful of steps to Melanie's front door, which opened before he could ring the bell. Melanie stood framed in the doorway. Her eyes were puffy and red-rimmed. Judging by the red blotches on Melanie's face, she looked as if she'd been crying all night.

"Come on in."

She was silent as she waited for him to take off his jacket. Hanging it on a hook, she turned to him. "Oh, Sam. I'm so sorry."

"What?"

She was sobbing in earnest now. "All this time, I blamed the accident all on you. But it was *my* fault. I'm so sorry, Sam."

He smoothed down her hair, wet with her tears. "It's okay. Calm down. It wasn't your fault," he said softly. "It was mine."

"But I remember now, Sam. All of it. Everything."

"Good," he said, not sure of exactly what she remembered, or if it actually *was* good.

"It's all been coming back. I must have blocked out the painful details."

She led him over to the couch and sat down next to him. Pouring him a cup of coffee from the pot sitting on a silver tray, she set it down. "Cream? Sugar?"

"Black."

He wanted to take her hand to comfort her. Whatever she was about to tell him, it had been preying on her mind.

She took a sip from her mug. "A while before the storm, I'd learned that Mike was cheating on me." Melanie paused, then brushed her hair back from her face. "We had a big fight, and he kept pouring himself drink after drink. Then the siren went off in the middle of everything. I told him that he wasn't in any condition to help, but he wouldn't listen."

She closed her eyes. "You know the rest. I slipped on the ice and hit my head, and woke up in the hospital a while later."

He shook his head. "I tried to talk to you at the hospital, but was advised against it."

"You tried to talk to me?"

"Yes."

"And here I thought you'd just left town."

"I'd never do that," he said.

"I know that now." She looked down at her hands. "I think I knew near the end that Mike was cheating on me. He was getting careless— almost as if he wanted me to find out."

When she lifted her eyes to look at him, they were bright with tears. "You see, Sam, it was so much easier to blame everything on you than to face the fact that my marriage was a sham." She sighed. "I should have tried harder to stop him."

Sam shook his head. "He was a big boy, Melanie. You did what you could." He took a deep breath and let it out. "I thought I smelled liquor on his breath, but when I questioned him, he told me he had only had one drink to warm up. I believed him. Even so, I should have sent him home. After a while, I knew his coordination was off. I realized that he had had more than one drink. Much more. I finally yelled at him to climb down, but he probably couldn't hear me over the noise of the generators and all. Then it was too late."

Sam looked down at the carpet, and Melanie could tell he was reliving that day.

"I treated you horribly," she whispered, holding his face in her hands. "No more, Sam. Mike made his choices, and we aren't going to blame ourselves anymore."

Melanie moved closer to him, and realized that she *wanted* to kiss him. Badly.

Holding hands, they sat in silence for a while, until Sam finally asked, "How do you feel?"

"Lighter, much lighter. Happier. Relieved."

"Good. So do I." He pulled her toward him and studied her face.

She knew what he was going to do, and she couldn't resist, didn't want to resist.

"Melanie?" Her name was like a whisper on his lips. He was asking permission, giving her time to say no.

"Yes?" she whispered, moving closer to him.

His lips touched hers, soft and tentative, but she wanted more. Putting her arms around his neck, she pulled him closer.

He made a low, guttural sound, and that excited her.

He deepened the kiss, teasing his lips with his tongue until she opened for him. He took that as an invitation to plunge deeper, to pull her even closer to his strong chest.

Melanie didn't want it to end. She wanted more, heaven help her, but finally she came to her senses and gently pulled back.

Wrapped in his strong arms, she felt safe and cherished. Above all, she felt desirable—something she hadn't felt in a long time.

She rested her head on his shoulder and let herself enjoy the movement of his hand through her hair. She would remember this moment for a lifetime, but she wouldn't—couldn't—let it happen again.

Because as much as she wanted to acknowledge her attraction to Sam, she knew she'd never be able to trust her heart to another man.

Chapter Seven

Later that morning, Sam drove to Utica, re-hashing his conversation with Melanie and thinking about the way she'd reacted to his kiss.

He didn't know what had made him kiss her. Maybe it was just because he'd wanted to since he'd first met her at the tree lighting, before he even knew who she was.

He could still feel a heated rush when he thought of the feel of her soft lips. If he hadn't reined himself in and left when he had, they'd be in bed together right now.

But it wasn't the right time, and he whole-heartedly wanted things to be perfect if—when—they made love.

Pulling into the parking lot, he hurried into the store. With a clerk in tow to guide him, he scooped up every possible Katie Ann item he could find along with wrapping paper and bows and was back in Hawk's Lake in time for the snowman-making contest.

There was no sign of Melanie, so when Kyle asked him to be the fourth member of his team, along with his two uncles, Sam jumped at the chance. They made a huge snowman and used stones for his eyes, mouth and nose. Brian had donated a flannel shirt and Jack had a snow-brush to place in the snowman's twig hand. Sam had a red baseball cap for the snowman's head.

They didn't win, but they had plenty of laughs, a snowball fight, and they made angels in the snow. Sam had a terrific time with Kyle. He was a great kid—smart and a lot of fun.

Kyle was excited to be playing hockey in the "big game" at the Snow Festival, and that was all he could talk about. Sam didn't tell him that he was going to be one of the referees, even though he was almost as excited as Kyle to be lacing up and getting back on the ice. It had been a long time.

The loud motors and diesel smell of tractors pulling hay wagons overpowered the laughter and chatter of everyone waiting in line for a ride to Tucker's Pond for the hockey game. Sam and Kyle joined the Hawkins brothers, who were helping people into the wagons.

"Have you seen my mom yet?" Kyle asked his uncles, scanning the crowd. Then he pointed. "Oh, there she is."

Melanie hurried toward them. Just looking at her, Sam felt hot all over again. When she looked his way, she smiled and waved, and he thought he noticed a blush on her cheeks.

"Did you win, Kyle?" she asked, squatting down to talk to Kyle at eye level.

"Nope." He shook his head. "But we made a real cool snowman."

"That's great, sweetie. I'm sorry I overslept, but I'm sure it was great. Right now we'd better get to the hockey game. I brought your gear." She placed a red and gold gym bag onto the wagon.

"Thanks, Mom." Kyle scrambled into the wagon.

Sam held out a hand to help Melanie up the steps positioned in front of the wagon, and she took it, thanking him with a smile.

"Well, Sleeping Beauty finally arises," Jack chided as he climbed in behind her. "Get a good sleep?"

"After a while," she said, making her way to one of the hay bales.

Sam was last to get on.

"We've got room over here," Jack yelled, pointing to a six-inch space next to Melanie. "Move over, Mel."

She raised an eyebrow at Jack, but moved over as much as possible so Sam could squeeze into the small space.

"Excited about the game, partner?" Brian asked Kyle.

Kyle shrugged, playing it cool.

"Did you get any tips from Mr. LeDoux?" Jack cocked a thumb at Sam.

Kyle furrowed his brows. "Huh?"

"Don't you know that he's Sam 'The Slammer' LeDoux?" Jack gave the boy a sly grin. "He played for the Canucks."

Kyle's eyes widened. "You are? You did?"

"Everyone in Canada plays hockey." He laughed. "But seriously, I played for the Canucks a long time ago. They recruited me after high school. It was just something I had to try. Then I blew my knee, and my career was over," Sam explained. "But it gave me the money to go to college for what I do now."

"But you were a Canuck? That's my favorite team of all teams!"

"Mine, too," Sam said. "The Ducks are weenies." He stole a glance at Melanie, remembering that only a couple of days ago she'd chastised him for laughing. Now, he was rewarded with a big smile.

"Yeah," said Kyle. "The Ducks are weenies."

The two of them high-fived, their bond now secure.

The wagons turned right and down a slight grade to what Sam assumed was the Tucker place. A fairly large frozen pond was off to the right, complete with markings and nets. The only thing lacking was a wood-and-clear plastic barrier, which was probably why they only let the peewees play. Otherwise, the spectators would have to worry about keeping their teeth.

Hay bales covered with Army blankets were lined up on both sides of the ice, stretching out like long caterpillars. Three big tents bustled with people, and a row of royal-blue portable toilets stood like soldiers to the right.

"This is really something," he said to Melanie.

"Everyone loves the Snow Festival," she replied. "It gets us through the long winter."

"It's wonderful."

When the wagon stopped, Sam hopped down and began helping the passengers off. Cal approached to lend a hand.

"Amazing, isn't it?" Cal asked, nodding at the rink.

Sam raised an eyebrow when he noticed a Zamboni rolling in to smooth the ice. Clearly the people of Hawk's Lake took their hockey as seriously as the people of Lenore.

"You're not kidding. I never expected this," Sam said. "A Zamboni?"

"You betcha." Cal laughed. "We do it up right for the big peewee game."

Sam helped Melanie down from the tractor, feeling his body react to her as she slid to the ground. He wanted to keep her in his arms for a little while, but she smiled briefly at him and hurried away with Kyle.

After everyone was unloaded, he walked toward the various tents that were to his right, where some people were selling crafts. His gaze was drawn to the quilts on display. His mother would love one, and it would make a perfect Christmas present.

He looked at the Hawkins family gathered together to watch Kyle play and remembered a time when his family was as close as theirs. That was before they sold their farm and land in Lenore to a developer, and they all moved to different places in the States.

Sam gripped his friend's shoulder. "You live

in a wonderful town, Cal. It's a great place to raise a family."

"I know," Cal grinned, looking over at his own little family. "There's a lot of heart in Hawk's Lake."

Sam's heart was still in Lenore, which was partly why he never settled anywhere. No place was ever as good.

Sam scanned the crowd for Melanie, and spotted her sitting with her brothers and father at centerline, ready for the face-off.

Just then, Melanie looked in his direction. In that moment, across the cold air, something crackled between them. He wondered if she'd felt it, too.

He would have liked nothing better than to sit shoulder to shoulder, thigh to thigh next to her and enjoy the game, but duty called.

As Sam walked with Cal toward the tents, the smell of hot dogs, hamburgers and popcorn drifted on the crisp breeze. People were already lined up to purchase food and sitting at picnic tables, both inside and outside the tents.

"We'd better change," Cal told him, checking his watch. "It's face-off in a half hour. I hope you have thermal underwear on."

"Of course," Sam snorted. He was no stranger to the cold.

"Good. I just figured that living in that tropical climate of Montreal, you'd turned into a surfer."

Sam laughed. "I can still outskate you any day."

That was a bluff. It had been a long time since he'd skated and he was going to need some warm-up time—a lot of it. He didn't want to make a fool of himself in front of the crowd. Or Melanie Bennett.

He glanced back at Melanie, catching her gaze. For a moment he saw the interested speculation in her expression instead of the ghosts of their shared tragedy.

Now they could move on, Sam thought, and take their relationship to the next level. And he was going to do whatever it took to make that happen.

Chapter Eight

For Melanie, the first period of Kyle's championship game wasn't half as exciting as watching Sam LeDoux on the ice.

When the game began, Melanie couldn't take her eyes off Sam's powerful thighs, outlined by the thin fabric of his black pants as he skated. His arms were just as powerful in the stretchy black-and-white-striped referee's jacket as he plucked the peewees off each other whenever they piled up and set them back on their feet.

Above all, she enjoyed how his blue eyes sparkled with humor as he tried not to laugh at some of the antics of the players.

Right now, one of the Polar Bears was standing in front of his mother as she wiped his nose with a tissue. Two of the Glaciers were making snow angels on the ice. Then one of the Polar Bears—number seven—raised his hand and yelled to Sam that he had to go to the bathroom.

Kyle was number seven.

Sam blew his whistle for the end of first quarter. Kyle skated to the portable toilets as fast as he could, as Sam skated toward Melanie.

"They are totally out of control." Sam chuckled as he executed a perfect hockey stop. "But I'm having the time of my life. It reminds me of my coaching days."

"You used to coach?" Melanie asked. She could picture it easily. From what she'd already witnessed at the library the other day, he was wonderful with kids, patient and kind.

"A Canuck pal recruited me into helping him with the Lenore Lasers high-school team for a couple of years—just on weekends. I loved it, but I had to step aside when I was appointed a relief delegate for the Red Cross and had to travel all over the world at a moment's notice."

She lowered her eyes, focusing on the ice.

"Yeah, I know," Sam said. "I get the same re-action all the time whenever I mention disaster or tell people what I do. But if it's any consolation, for the past year I've relegated myself to just volunteering."

"You're not on call anymore?"

"No. I needed a break from management for a while." He looked over his shoulder. "I'd better get back on the ice. It looks like we're almost ready to start."

Something in his expression told her he wasn't telling the truth, or at least not the whole truth.

She could understand how his job would be taxing. He had to have seen a lot of destruction in his line of work.

Melanie watched him skate back to the center of the ice. She'd never considered that Sam's life might have changed after the ice storm, too. Everyone said he was the best in the business, but now he was working for others instead of managing his own teams.

That was quite a shift in responsibility for such a take-charge man.

Cal Lippert blew the whistle, bringing her face back to the game. The peewees wobbled back onto the ice. Melanie was glad that the periods had been shortened or the kids would have been too exhausted to enjoy the rest of the evening.

Melanie watched Sam shepherd the kids

into place and tried to convince herself that she wasn't attracted to him. They simply had a history together—an unfortunate incident that had made their paths cross. She didn't want to get to know him any more or admire him. And she definitely didn't want to care about him. Yet her heart did a little flip as she thought of the kisses they'd shared earlier—kisses that rocked her down to her toes.

She didn't want another man in her life. She wanted to be alone with her son, as usual.

How could she ever trust a man again?

Back from the portable toilet, Kyle raced toward the rink. The coach and town dentist, John Denton, caught him before he skated onto the ice, leaned over and talked to him. Kyle nodded and began to put the goalie equipment on. Kyle didn't particularly like being a goalie—it required him staying put for the most part—but he was a good sport.

For the entire second period, Kyle stood in front of the goal. Then sat in front of it. Then lay on his stomach in front of it. The game never came near him. By the time the whistle blew, Melanie was holding back rueful laughter.

The third and last period was coming up. Mothers and fathers were at the ready to change gloves, blow noses and pass out cocoa and bottles of water. Melanie watched as Coach Denton tried unsuccessfully to get the kids' attention for a little pep talk. Thankfully, Kyle didn't have to be goalie anymore. His friend Freddie Kilmartin was putting the gear on.

Coach Denton blew his whistle three times. "Polar Bears, we have only five minutes before this game is over. We are going to win this thing. Now sit down and listen up."

The score was zero to zero, so it was anyone's game. Sam and Cal Lippert were entertaining the crowd by doing intricate maneuvers with their sticks and the puck. Sam effortlessly flew around the ice as if he had been born on it. The wind ruffled his jet-black hair as he skated back and forth.

His cheeks, nose and the tips of his ears were red. He should be wearing a hat, Melanie thought absently, and then caught herself. Why did she care if he wore a hat or not? She wasn't his mother, and he certainly wasn't looking at her as if she were. It had been a long time since a man had looked at her the way Sam did.

Was she willing to admit—to herself, anyway—that she cared about Sam? That she was concerned about him?

The answer to both questions was a resounding *yes*.

Her attraction to Sam had come upon her so suddenly and she'd fought it. But she could no longer deny that she liked his looks, his smile, the masculine aura about him.

For her to admit to that was like a shock to her senses. But she wouldn't let it go anywhere.

She could like him without falling for him. They could be friends. That's all.

Yeah, right.

Sam checked his watch. There were about three minutes left in the game and he couldn't wait until it was over. His old hockey injuries were aggravating him, and he was using muscles that he'd forgotten he had.

He wished someone—anyone—would make a goal.

Right now, a Polar Bear and a Glacier were smashing sticks as if they were in a sword fight. The puck sat on the ice in front of them.

Kyle came skating out of nowhere. He took a swing at the puck and it went flying toward the Glaciers' goalie, who was busy sucking the snow off his gloves. The puck ran out of steam, but another Polar Bear sent it flying right toward Melanie.

Luckily, Sam was close, since Melanie was

talking to her brother Brian and didn't notice the puck zooming right toward her head.

Sam leapt into the air, arm outstretched. He couldn't quite reach it, but Jack's hand seemed to shoot out of nowhere, snatching the puck.

Unfortunately, Sam couldn't stop.

His forward momentum tipped Melanie over on her hay bale, and he found himself stretched out on top of her. Her eyes were wide with shock, her dark eyelashes a glossy fringe around them. Her lips formed a perfect circle.

"Are you okay?" he asked. He could feel her breasts against his chest even through layers of insulation. With her stretched out under him, he could tell they'd fit together perfectly. He wanted to take her into his arms and taste her lips, inhale the fresh air on her skin.

He wanted to make love to her until she cried out in pleasure.

She blinked. "Wh-what happened?"

Sam studied the snow on the ends of her hair to distract his brain. "The puck was coming straight at you. A wild shot."

He stared at her lips again. They had come together in a slight smile. It would be so easy to bend his head and touch his mouth to hers…

Someone cleared his throat, and Sam felt a

hand grip his left arm, then another grip his right arm.

"Need help getting up, Sam?" Jack asked.

He was set back on his feet by the Hawkins brothers, who helped Melanie up next and righted her hay bale. Sam still felt dazed as he looked at her. She was blushing. He glanced at the smiling crowd around them.

Jack handed him the puck. "They're waiting for this, ref."

Sam closed his hand around the puck and skated back onto the ice. Cal made his way toward Sam.

"You okay?"

Sam let out a deep breath. "Yeah."

"Can you keep your mind on the peewees for three minutes, loverboy?"

Sam was about to shoot a smart remark in Cal's direction when someone skated into Sam's leg.

"Ow." Sam rubbed the spot and moved away from the offending peewee, Kyle.

Worried eyes stared up at him. "Sam, is my mom hurt?"

"She's fine." At least he hoped she was. "So, how about if we finish this game?"

"Yeah." Kyle skated toward the rest of the

Polar Bears who had begun a snowball fight during the lull. "Come on, guys. Let's win."

The Polar Bears skated onto the ice, and the Glaciers followed. Cal blew his whistle twice. "Face off."

The entire town was thrilled that the Hawk's Lake Polar Bears won by one goal. Cheers echoed across the pretty little valley and could probably be heard all the way to Lake Placid, Melanie thought.

There were more cheers during the trophy presentation when Mayor Lippert announced that the trophy would be on display at the town hall, proclaimed the day as Polar Bear Day and invited the two teams for all the hot dogs and cocoa that they wanted. But Melanie wasn't prepared for his next announcement.

"I'd like to present two special guests," he said. "Russ and Noreen Bennett, the parents of our late friend, Mike Bennett."

"Grandma and Grandpa are here?" Kyle's eyes were wide. "Cool."

"I didn't know they were coming," Melanie stammered. Her stomach filled with butterflies. This couldn't be good. It never was when Noreen and Russ showed up. "I thought they were in Palm Springs for the winter."

"Interesting." Melanie's father frowned and whispered, "Wonder what they're up to."

"I think we're about to find out, Dad."

Noreen swept up the stairs in an ankle-length white fur, which Melanie hoped was fake, but she doubted it. She had on a matching cowboy-style hat that she wore at a jaunty angle. The stylish ensemble was probably lost on the crowd who sported either red plaid hunting jackets or puffy, quilted parkas.

Russ Bennett was as distinguished as ever in a cashmere camel coat. He looked every bit the head of a multimillion-dollar hotel empire.

Russ had wanted his son to follow in his footsteps, and Noreen had blamed Melanie for keeping him in Hawk's Lake, among other things.

Russ Bennett took the microphone from Cal. "Thank you, Mayor Lippert." His gaze swept the audience. "Will Melanie and Kyle please join us?"

Reluctantly, Melanie took Kyle's hand and walked toward her in-laws. She had no idea what was coming and she hated surprises.

The Bennetts had pretty much ignored her throughout her marriage to their son, and she'd barely heard from them after his death. So what were they doing here?

She did appreciate the fact that they always remembered Kyle on his birthdays and Christmas, even though they lavished him with expensive presents too advanced for his age level and flew him out to Palm Springs for two weeks when school let out. Only recently had she convinced them to buy him smaller gifts and begin a college fund for him instead.

Noreen gave her a couple of air kisses and bent down to hug Kyle. Blanketed in white fur, Kyle practically disappeared. Melanie heard him sneeze a moment later.

Russ Bennett gave him a stiff handshake. "Hello, Kyle."

"Hi, Grandpa."

"Melanie." He shook her hand.

"Russ."

"I'll bet you're wondering what this is about," he said.

"Definitely."

There was nothing heartwarming about Mike's parents, nothing at all. She tolerated them for Kyle's sake, and they tolerated her. She hadn't forced Mike into marrying her, but they'd never believed that.

All she'd done was answer a call for a tow that came into the garage one day. When she arrived with the tow truck, Mike Bennett had been fascinated by the fact that she was a mechanic. She'd checked out his school-bus-yellow Mustang. All it needed was a new fan belt, so she'd towed it to the garage and put one in.

But Mike hadn't let it end there. He asked her to dinner. He took her boating on the lake. On their third date, in the room above his parents' boathouse, she'd slept with him. It was romantic and wonderful and deliciously forbidden. She'd always assumed that she'd gotten pregnant when they made love for the third time that evening, when they'd been so caught up that they'd forgotten to use a condom.

What Melanie hadn't known then—and what seemed to have slipped Mike's mind—was the fact that he was engaged to Donna McSwain, whose parents owned a big mail-order firm that sold everything from perfume to tractors.

Mike had sworn that Donna was old news, that he loved Melanie. When they announced their engagement, both the McSwains and the Bennetts were outraged. Their great merger was over before it even began.

Instead of an heiress for a daughter-in-law, the Bennetts got Melanie Hawkins, grease monkey. They never thought she was good enough for Mike and made that as clear as fine crystal.

"As you know," Russ Bennett began, addressing the crowd, "it was almost a year ago that we lost our son, Mike, in a terrible accident. In Mike's memory, I would like to announce that my wife and I are going to fund several scholarships for deserving high school seniors in the area."

Cheers went up from the crowd.

Melanie had to admit that the scholarships were a nice gesture. The students in the small villages scattered throughout the Adirondacks would certainly benefit from them.

Russ rambled on, talking about his vision for the scholarships. Melanie noticed people shuffling on their feet in the cold. The sun was starting to set, and they wanted to eat, shop for crafts and warm up by the bonfire.

"And we'd like our daughter-in-law, Melanie Bennett, to oversee the scholarship program. Melanie?"

She jumped when she heard her name. Russ took that as a yes and nodded to her.

Then he handed the microphone back to Mayor Lippert.

"Thank you very much. This is very generous of you. Let's have a big round of applause for Russ and Noreen Bennett."

There was more hooting and hollering. Mayor Lippert raised his hands and the crowd became silent. "Now, grab a bite to eat and enjoy the free skate. The bonfire will be lit at six o'clock followed by the singing of Christmas carols. Thank you everyone." He clicked off the microphone.

Russ leaned over to Kyle. "Kyle, how about if we take you out to dinner? Then you can stay overnight at our hotel. We have a big suite."

Noreen put a gloved hand on his cheek. "And we have a present for you, sweetie."

Russ straightened and turned toward Melanie. "Of course, you're welcome to join us. We're staying at Conifer Cliffs. They have a five-star restaurant there."

Melanie knew she was asked only as an afterthought, and that neither of them sincerely wanted her to join them. They just wanted to visit with Kyle.

"Actually, Kyle and I planned on staying here and enjoying the free skate and the bonfire. We had no idea that you were going to be in town."

"The mayor wanted it to be a surprise."

"We have to leave tomorrow," Noreen said, crossing her arms. "I'd like to spend some time with my grandson."

There was a time when Melanie would have backed down to keep the peace, but no more. "You're welcome to join us here for hot dogs and burgers and the bonfire after. It's not five-star like the restaurant at Conifer Cliffs, but it's at least a one-star." She tried to joke, but the Bennetts didn't crack a smile.

Kyle stood between them, looking from his grandparents to his mother, and her heart broke a little bit. It wasn't fair of Russ and Noreen to spring such an invite on him on such a special night.

"I'm kind of tired from the hockey game, Mom," Kyle said politely. "I'd rather go with Grandma and Grandpa."

Tired? One look at Kyle's bright eyes told her that he was lying through his teeth in an effort to be nice to his grandparents, and she loved him for that.

"Are you sure, sweetie? I thought you wanted to hang out with the Polar Bears."

"That's okay, Mom. I'd like to stay at the hotel overnight. It's a real cool place, and they have a pool."

"Well, then go for it and have a great time."

Melanie knew that it was killing her son to pass up the bonfire and celebration with his team, but despite her frustration she was proud of him for doing and saying the right thing.

She forced herself to smile. "Kyle, get your duffel. I packed some extra clothes in it just in case you got wet from the game, so you're good to go. Have a great time."

He ran off to the tent that was serving as a locker room.

She stood with her in-laws in silence. Nothing she wanted to say to them would improve the situation. Let them continue to think that Mike was perfect, and that she had ruined his life. She knew otherwise.

"Kyle is such a good-natured boy. You're doing a wonderful job with him, Melanie," Russ said.

"Thank you." Melanie knew her voice sounded stiff, but she couldn't help being suspicious. "I appreciate you saying that."

"He'd do wonders at the Hudson prep school where Michael went," Noreen said. "He could meet another class of people, broaden his horizons and get out of these godforsaken mountains."

Outrage rippled through Melanie. "Prep school? Not a chance. He's my son, and he's staying here with me. He's only six years old, for heaven's sake."

"But—"

Russ held his hand up. "Noreen, I told you not to bring that up now."

"I'd appreciate if you never brought it up

again—ever," Melanie said, adamantly. "It's not going to happen."

The Bennetts acted like they didn't hear her.

Melanie barely listened to their strained small talk as they all walked toward the Bennetts' rental car. All she could think was that Kyle would stay right here in Hawk's Lake with his family and friends.

Then it occurred to her that she'd be alone at Sunshine Cottage tonight.

Melanie searched for Sam and saw several of the players talking to him. Looking up, he spotted her and once again, it was as if everyone else faded away. She waved, and tried to calm the flutters in her stomach.

She knew she'd never marry again, but maybe there was nothing wrong with a little flirtation, or even a date. Maybe she'd invite Sam over for dinner.

Excitement skittered through her body, and she felt a definite pull toward him.

And Melanie wondered if she really wanted to stop herself and just be friends, as she'd just resolved, or jump right in, enjoy herself—and remember what it was like to be with a man.

Chapter Nine

Melanie waved goodbye to Kyle as he drove off with his grandparents.

They'd promised to drop him off tomorrow at Hawk's Roost, the magnificent lake house that had been in the Hawkins family for decades. She'd meet them there at noon.

Every holiday, the entire family gathered there, along with relatives and friends. Her father was quick to find anyone who might be alone for Thanksgiving or Christmas and invite them for dinner, too.

Just yesterday, she'd told Kyle that they should move into The Roost the week before Christmas. Kyle had several days off from school, and

Melanie thought they could make a little vacation of it. They could put up their Christmas tree there, hang lights and decorate the place inside and out. Hawk's Roost would be extra festive this year.

They could snowshoe and cross-country ski and skate on the frozen lake, right outside their door. They'd make snowmen, have snowball fights and eat popcorn as they watched Christmas movies in front of the tree. They'd have a wonderful week together, just the two of them. Then they would share dinner with everyone on Christmas Eve, as well as the next day.

Speaking of dinner, Melanie decided to have a bite to eat at the food tent before heading home. Once inside, she saw her brother Jack surrounded by a bevy of women, as usual. Around the perimeter of women stood a ring of boys armed with paper and pens, hoping for an opening in the circle to scoot in and get Jack's autograph. If she knew her brother, he'd stay all night to sign and talk to the kids.

Brian had a similar circle of women around him—the academic, moneyed circle.

That left her father. Maybe she could sit with him and they could keep each other company.

Famished, she ordered a hamburger and a hot dog, along with a cup of coffee. Balancing everything on a thin cardboard tray, she proceeded through the slushy snow, mud and hay covering the old carpeting in the center of the tent, looking for her dad—and found him sitting with Sam. She thought yet again of their kiss, and her heart did another one of those annoying flips.

The two of them were deep in conversation and looked tighter than two coats of paint. Finally, Ed spotted her and waved her over.

Sam stood, took her tray, and pulled out a chair for her.

Ed cleared his throat. "Mel, is it true that you're letting Kyle spend the night with the Bennetts?"

"Ah…the Hawk's Lake eavesdroppers are at work again. Yes, it's true, and Kyle already left with them."

"Humph."

"He deserves to know his grandparents."

Ed crushed his coffee cup in one hand. "Where were they when you and Mike got married?"

Melanie rolled her eyes at the tired subject. "You know the answer to that, Dad."

Ed turned to Sam. "They were protesting. That's what they were doing. They never came to the wedding."

Sam sat back in his chair. "That's unfortunate. I'm sure that cast a shadow over the event."

Ed leaned forward. "I'll tell you why they didn't come."

"Dad!" Melanie shot her father a don't-you-dare look.

Sam held up his hands and chuckled. "Ed, Melanie seems uncomfortable with this conversation."

Melanie appreciated Sam's thoughtfulness, but it was hopeless. Once her father got his jaws flapping, there was no stopping him. She sighed.

"My daughter was the injured party," Ed continued, as if he hadn't heard either of them. "Melanie was pregnant with Kyle. The Bennetts said that she'd ruined Mike's life, and that she got pregnant to trap him because he was a good catch."

Hearing that statement again made Melanie just as sick as the first time. Russ and Noreen didn't know the truth about their son or about their marriage. He was never a good husband or a good father. Though he'd loved Kyle in his own way, he certainly hadn't loved her—not enough to stay faithful.

She looked pointedly at her father. "It was a long time ago. Russ and Noreen adore Kyle, so that's all that matters. I'm not going to keep their only grandchild away from them."

"What's this I hear about them wanting Kyle to go to some prep school?" her father asked.

She raised an eyebrow. This town's grapevine was unbelievable.

"What did you tell them?"

"I told them no, of course."

"Did they get the message?"

"If they didn't, I'll keep telling them until they do." Melanie wanted this discussion over. "Dad, let's not bore Sam with old history."

"This is new history." Ed drummed his fingers on the table, then turned to Sam. "Sorry, Sam. My daughter doesn't want me to discuss her, and I try to do what she wants."

Sam laughed. "In my experience, if Melanie doesn't want to talk about something, she means it."

"Would *you* want *your* son to go to a prep school?" Ed asked Sam.

Sam hesitated for several seconds, then looked at Melanie. "No. I wouldn't. As far as I'm concerned, Melanie, you did absolutely the right thing."

Melanie smiled at him. She appreciated his support, not that she needed it, but she appreciated it anyway. And it was time to let Sam off the hook and change the subject.

"Speaking of home, Sam, what was your

home like in Canada when you were growing up?"

His face relaxed and his eyes grew even brighter, and Melanie could tell he was going back to a good time in his life.

"We had a dairy farm," he said. "There was lots of work, but what I remember most was the big kitchen in our house, just like your house, Melanie. My friends were always welcome, and the kitchen table was the center for homework, heated political debates and intense discussions about hockey—all of which were accompanied by my mom's lemonade or my dad's home-brewed beer, depending on the season and the age of the visitors."

Melanie noticed Sam's eyes dim, and his smile fade. "What happened?"

He shrugged. "Things changed a few years ago. My parents sold the farm, and they retired to a senior community in Florida. The land was developed into condos for summer residents. Our big red barn now stores mowing equipment and golf carts for a private golf course. The homestead is a B & B owned by someone from Kentucky."

"Where's your family now?"

"All over the place. My brother, Jean-Luc, is a world-class skier. He's training for the Olympics in Park City, Utah. My sister, Michelle, is in Los Angeles, writing for a sitcom."

"Aren't you getting together for Christmas?" she asked.

"Not this year. We usually all head down to Florida, but this year my folks are taking a tour of Europe with a group of their friends for Christmas and New Year."

"How wonderful!" Melanie said.

"The dairy farm always tied them down, so now they're eager to explore the world." Sam smiled. "The trip is our combination Christmas and fortieth anniversary present to them. After they return, we're all going to get together in Florida to hear about their trip and celebrate a belated Christmas."

But that meant that Sam would spend Christmas alone. She couldn't imagine the holidays without her family.

"By the way, Melanie," Ed cut in to the conversation. "I suggested that Sam move into Hawk's Roost while he's here."

Melanie couldn't have heard him correctly. "What did you say, Dad?"

She saw Sam wince, then concentrate on his coffee. He must have picked up on the edge in her voice.

"Why should Sam pay for a hotel room when

The Roost is empty?" Ed asked. "And now that I know that his family probably isn't getting together for Christmas, I'm inviting him to move into The Roost right away and to spend Christmas with all of us." He turned to Sam. "What's your answer, Sam?"

All her Christmas plans with Kyle evaporated into the frosty air. "But, Dad, I—"

"You'll like Hawk's Roost, Sam." Ed sat up a little taller in his folding chair. "It's the perfect place to kick back and relax in between grand marshal duties." Ed laughed. "And if I say so myself, Christmas is a special time there."

Her father turned to Melanie, continuing as if she hadn't even spoken. "I figured Sam could help Kyle with his hockey game. The lake is perfect for skating."

"I'd love to help Kyle with his game," Sam said, with a careful smile. "Whether or not I take you up on your gracious invitation."

Melanie restrained herself from banging on the table in frustration. "But Dad, Kyle and I were going to—"

Ed continued to talk as if she wasn't trying to get a word in.

Sam was watching her intently. Even if her father was oblivious to the fact that she was irritated, Sam seemed quite aware. "Ed, I think Melanie is trying to tell you something," he said.

Melanie gave him a grateful glance and turned to her father. "Yes, I am."

"Well, what's stopping you? Speak up."

He was so frustrating. At this point, there was no sense telling him that *she* had plans to be at Hawk's Roost during Christmas week. It was her father's place, and he could invite whomever he wanted. She should have told her father of her plans sooner, but now it was too late. Sam was in and she was out.

She sighed. "Never mind, Dad. Forget it."

One bright spot was that Kyle would have bragging rights at school. No Polar Bear had ever had personal hockey lessons from a former member of the Canucks. That would mean an extra-special Christmas for Kyle, which was just what she'd wanted for him anyway.

She smiled at Sam. "Kyle would be thrilled to take hockey lessons from you, Sam. That's very generous of you."

"My pleasure." Sam smiled back at her, and it warmed her down to her cold toes.

It had been so much easier to dislike him. It would be so easy to fall for him, too. But she just couldn't let herself fall into that trap again.

"Ed, I really appreciate the invite to spend

Christmas with your family. And I'll definitely give some thought to staying at Hawk's Roost." He turned toward Melanie. "How about if we sit awhile at the bonfire?"

She nodded, blaming her acceptance on her cold feet and hands and not on the fact that she tingled at the idea of being alone with Sam.

He smiled and turned to her father. "Ed, you're welcome to join us."

"You two go ahead. Diane Henderson asked me to sit with her," Ed said. "Maybe I'll get lucky tonight."

Melanie laughed, even as she groaned. It was hard to stay mad at her father for long.

Ed drifted off to find his friend, leaving Melanie alone with Sam.

"Shall we?" Sam asked.

"Sure."

Sam stood, took her tray with all the litter and disposed of it. Then he pulled out her chair and held out his arm.

With only a slight hesitation, she threaded her arm through his.

Sam scanned the area around the bonfire for a couple of unoccupied hay bales. The wind had picked up and the temperature had probably dropped a good ten degrees. A light snow was falling, but not enough to make things uncomfortable.

They straightened out a green Army blanket and draped it evenly over the bales. They sat down, and Sam could immediately feel the heat from the bonfire. He stretched out so his boots could be closer to the fire, and Melanie did the same. His arms brushed hers, and he wondered what she'd do if he held her hand.

Over the snapping of the wood and the hiss of the flames, they could only hear the murmur of the other people around them.

They didn't talk for a while, content to watch the flames flicker against the dark winter sky.

"Your father is quite a character," Sam finally said.

"He has a knack for embarrassing people. I'm sorry if it made you uncomfortable. So now that you know all about me, it's your turn. Any skeletons in your closet?" Melanie asked.

"No. I've lived a very dull life. The Red Cross keeps things exciting."

Melanie took another Army blanket and draped it over their legs. "So, what made you become a disaster response expert?"

"An avalanche."

"How?"

"When I was in college, I was skiing in the

Canadian Rockies in British Columbia with a group of my pals. Some of them skied where they shouldn't have and triggered an avalanche. They were hotshots. Stupid."

He still shuddered at the memory. "I had no idea that they would actually cross the warning signs. I tried to talk them out of it, but they called me chicken and took off. I couldn't do anything but yell after them to stop."

He didn't speak for a few long minutes, and Melanie knew he was thinking about that day, wondering if he could have done more. "Sam, are you okay?"

He turned back to her with an apologetic smile. "Sorry."

"How did it turn out with your friends?"

He shook his head. "I helped the rescuers bring their bodies out. From then on, I knew I wanted to do something in search and rescue. That eventually led to my job with the Red Cross."

"I'm so sorry you lost your friends." Her hand closed over his, and he liked how she was trying to comfort him.

"Thank you." He shook off the feeling as he tried to recall his buddies and the carefree days before the avalanche. "The experience changed me. After I quit the Canucks, I went to college, got a job with the Canadian Red Cross, and now I work as an international disaster response delegate."

"I'm sure you've seen a lot of destruction and sadness in the world."

"I've also seen happiness. People who are grateful for a second chance. I've seen the best in people."

Melanie's eyes filled with tears. "And the worst in people. Like me."

"That's not true." He squeezed her hand.

To his amazement, Melanie didn't pull her hand away. They sat in easy silence, hand-in-hand, listening to the crowd sing "Let it Snow." The bonfire crackled and sent little sparks into the air.

As the night progressed, Melanie yawned and eventually her head came to rest on his shoulder. He enjoyed just watching her as the flames made shadows dance across her face. She looked so peaceful, as if she didn't have a care in the world. Sam tried not to move so she wouldn't wake up.

But a woman's loud laughter jarred her awake.

"Oh. I didn't mean to fall asleep. I guess I should get home."

"I'll take you home."

"Stay and enjoy yourself. I can take the shuttle bus back to the parking lot by myself," she said. "I'll be fine."

Sam shook his head. "I'd rather be with you."

Her smile looked cautious although it warmed him down to his aching ankles and cold toes. He wondered what she thought of his bold statement and didn't care. Someone had to take a step beyond this skittish dance they were doing.

They walked up the incline to where a couple of school buses were waiting to take people back. Though the bus was empty, Sam motioned for Melanie to move in, and he sat next to her. His knees almost went through the back of the blue vinyl seat in front of him.

"Yeow. That hurts."

Melanie laughed, and he enjoyed the sound. It broke the tension that had hung between them like a thick fog. As he rubbed his kneecaps, he couldn't help but join in her laughter.

Their faces were close, her lashes long and wet with snowflakes. It wouldn't take much to dip his head and taste her lips.

The school bus jerked into action, and they were yanked back and forth in their seats as if riding a mechanical bull, and the moment was lost.

But not forgotten.

Chapter Ten

"Melanie, let me drive you home. You must be tired."

She didn't want to say good-night to Sam—not yet, anyway. "I'm fine. I seem to have gotten a second wind."

They stood in the parking lot at the village square talking, until they decided to move into Sam's truck to get out of the cold.

Sam unlocked the door and opened it to let her in.

Melanie looked at the boxes and bags piled on the front seat, on the floor, and in the back cab. "Uh…there's no room."

"Oops. I'm sorry. I forgot."

Melanie looked at the name of the store on the bags. "Looks like someone went shopping for toys. When on earth did you have time?"

"After I left your house this morning."

She grinned. He'd actually gone shopping for little Emily. The barrier around her heart crumbled a little, and she wanted to grab him and kiss him.

"Would you like me to help you wrap them before you take them to Mountain Lake Lodge?"

He grinned. "So much for being a Secret Santa."

"I couldn't help overhearing your conversation with Mrs. Farley at the library. Then you asked me where to find big toys." She pointed toward the boxes. "And these are certainly big toys."

"Okay. I'm busted." He held up his hands in surrender. "I probably could use some help." He pushed his hair back. "But they're at a hotel. What if they don't have a tree? I wanted Emily to see her presents all arranged."

"Reggie and Clara Cunningham—they're the owners of the Lodge—always make sure that any guest who wants a tree has one in their room. The rooms are huge there. You really should see the place, and there's no time like the present." She nudged him with her elbow. "*Present.* Get it?"

He didn't at first, but then he grinned. "Is that Melanie Bennett cracking a joke?"

Raising an eyebrow, she said, "Amazing, huh?"

"Yeah." He took out a package and motioned with his head. "I'll take you up on that offer, but you'll have to hold this and somehow try and get comfortable with the ones on the floor."

"No problem." Melanie climbed into the truck, put her seat belt on and took the package from him.

Sam started up the truck, and the window immediately frosted over. "How far away is this place anyway?"

"It's only eight miles down the main road, but it's a long eight miles due to the twist and turns. The road is clear, so there shouldn't be a problem unless there are drifts."

He waited until the windows defrosted, and they drove to the Lodge without a problem. Sam turned down the long driveway leading to the place and gave a long whistle. "This is amazing."

Each of the inn's numerous windows was aglow, casting light on the snow and the pines around it. Tiny white lights twinkled from the naked branches of trees that had shed their leaves months before. On the middle of the lawn stood a manger scene lit by several soft spotlights that gave it an ethereal glow.

"I love it here," Melanie said. "It's very... special."

Sam pulled into a parking area that was outlined in large, bright candy canes. Melanie could see into the lobby.

"That's Clara Cunningham. She'll keep your secret." She handed Sam the heavy package that had been on her lap. "You do your Secret Santa thing. I'll wait here."

Melanie watched as Sam knocked on the door, wiped his feet and then entered when Clara motioned for him to come in.

They had a conversation and Clara burst into a big smile. She nodded animatedly and pointed to a door off the lobby. They both walked over, and she opened the door and motioned for him to enter a small room. Sam made three more trips outside as Melanie shuttled the various-size bags to him.

Clara gave him a big hug and a kiss on the cheek, and a happy Sam got back into the truck where Melanie waited.

"She's going to tell Mrs. Farley in the morning that Secret Santa gifts arrived for Emily. Mrs. Farley can wrap them right in the room and hide them until Christmas morning."

"That's perfect, Sam!"

"I don't know who was more excited, Clara or me."

"I'm pretty excited myself," Melanie said. "You're going to make that little girl very happy."

Sam drove Melanie back to her car. Unwilling to part, they moved to the back of her Blazer where they sat like two tailgaters at a football game.

"I want to give Kyle the best Christmas I possibly can this year," she eventually told him.

"Is there anything I can do to help?"

"That's nice of you, Sam. I think he'd love those hockey lessons from a former Canuck, since the Canucks are his favorite team."

"Well, those Ducks are weenies, you know," he said.

They laughed.

"I also want to thank you for filling in for me at the snowman contest. I still can't believe I overslept," she said, shaking her head.

"It was my pleasure. We had a great time."

They sat in comfortable silence for a few minutes, until Melanie realized if she didn't pull herself away from Sam now, it would only get harder.

"Well, I'd better get going." She held out her hand. "Thanks for a great day."

He took her hand, but instead of shaking it, he pulled her toward him and kissed her slowly and gently.

It would have been so easy to let herself go, give herself over to the pleasure of the moment. But she couldn't. She had to avoid more impulsive kisses.

Melanie remembered the first kiss they shared, and the usual streak of excitement shot through her body and settled low inside her. That kiss might have started out as impulsive, but it became more intense, more meaningful.

And just as she had before, she knew she should move away so it wouldn't lead to something more, something for which she wasn't ready.

But when Sam moved away first, she wasn't surprised to find herself terribly disappointed.

It was impossible for Melanie to sleep when she finally went to bed. She kept thinking back to her conversation with Sam. To his kisses.

Stop it, she scolded herself. He was good company, but she wasn't interested in taking things further. She just wasn't willing to open her heart again.

She didn't know when she finally drifted off, but the sun streaming through the windows woke her up. She opened one sleepy eye and looked at the clock.

Noon!

She was supposed to meet the Bennetts and Kyle at Hawk's Roost at noon. She sprang out of bed and dialed the number at The Roost. No answer.

But Kyle knew where the key was hidden, she told herself. He could let himself in. The Bennetts certainly wouldn't leave him there alone, not a six-year-old.

Darn. What was Russ Bennett's cell phone number? And why hadn't they called her?

Melanie raced around her bedroom, yanking on her jeans and pulling a sweater over her nightshirt. She pulled on her heavy socks. Running into the kitchen, she grabbed her jacket, stuffed her feet into boots and rushed outside with her purse to the Blazer.

She opened the door, and wasn't prepared for the sight that greeted her. "Awww, shoot." It had snowed at least eight inches last night, and she had to shovel her car out. More time lost.

She started up the car, put the heat on high to thaw the icy window, and then proceeded to brush off the snow with a corn broom.

"I can't believe I overslept again," she yelled, throwing the broom onto the floor of the backseat. She switched to four-wheel drive and backed over the huge bank of snow that the plow had pushed into her driveway.

She lowered her speed under the limit when she passed through town. There were too many people milling about, but why so many, she wondered.

Then she remembered. Tomorrow was the start of the snowmobile races to be held on the other side of town. Her brothers were the organizers of that event and the races drew people from all over the Northeast.

It was a big fundraiser for the fire department. They were hoping to put the proceeds toward another ambulance to serve the area.

It was also good for the local economy. Thanks to the popularity of the festival, the local eateries and shops were filled with tourists, and the hotels and campgrounds were likely booked to capacity.

About twenty-five minutes later, she finally made the turn onto the long dirt driveway that would lead her to the lake. Someone had plowed it after the overnight snowfall. It had to have been one of her brothers, or even her father. Thank goodness she didn't have to walk in from the highway. It would have taken her forever.

Shaking her head, she sighed. She had lived

here all her life. How could she have forgotten about the possibility of snow when she'd told the Bennetts to meet her at Hawk's Roost? The roads to Sunshine Cottage would be cleaner. Then again, Conifer Cliffs was closer to Hawk's Roost.

And how could she have overslept again?

It was because of Sam.

She thought of how handsome he'd looked in the light of the bonfire—the shadows accentuating his cheekbones along with the dimple on the right side of his mouth. When he sang along to the Christmas carols in his low baritone, his deep voice vibrated right through her, causing all her nerve endings to tingle. When he delivered Emily's gifts, he was so darn cute.

And when he'd kissed her, he was impossible to resist.

She was so preoccupied thinking about Sam's smile that she slid past the turn into Hawk's Roost. She stopped and backed up.

Just like Sunshine Cottage, it always amazed her that such a beautiful piece of architecture was built by her ancestors and was still in her family.

It was built in the tradition of what had come to be called the "Great Camps of the Adirondacks," with thick logs and native rock fireplaces. Porches and balconies jutted out from all four stories. She loved the castlelike turret room that had once been a playroom, but was now a library. Numerous windows peeked through the pines and hemlocks down to the spring-fed lake.

As she pulled around to the lakeside, which was actually the front of the camp, she didn't see the Bennetts' car. Anger rose and settled in her throat. They couldn't have left Kyle alone. Could they?

She relaxed when she saw Jack's big white truck parked over by the porch. The plow blade on the front was caked with snow. Sam must have plowed, and was probably keeping an eye on Kyle. Her anger dissipated.

Getting out of the car, she heard the sound of laughter and the cracking sound of wood on wood. Hockey sticks. Out on the frozen lake, Kyle and Sam were playing a game of one-on-one.

As she watched Sam skate toward her son, she remembered that he was moving into The Roost. It certainly hadn't taken him very long to plow his way in and make himself at home. Not long at all.

Kyle and Sam waved to her. As she walked over to the frozen lake, she couldn't help but notice how Sam's heavy fisherman's sweater outlined his broad shoulders. He wore faded jeans that clung perfectly to his strong thighs as he moved the puck back and forth toward Kyle.

"Hi, Mom," Kyle said, hardly sparing her a glance in favor of the rubber puck.

"Hi, sweetie. Hello, Sam. Sorry I'm late. I overslept again. Must be all the fresh air from last night."

"No harm done." Sam grinned. "Kyle and I are having a great time."

"Grandma and Grandpa Bennett had to leave, so they left me with Sam," Kyle said. "They said to say goodbye to you, and that they'll call you about the scholarships."

"Okay." Melanie pushed back a tangle of hair from her face. She hadn't had time to even brush it. She pulled out a knitted hat from the pocket of her coat and stuffed her hair inside. "And thanks for plowing, Sam."

He shrugged like he hadn't had to get up at the crack of dawn to do it. Didn't that man ever sleep?

"No problem," he said.

"Grandma and Grandpa got me a new hockey stick. Sam helped me tape it. Cool, huh?"

"Very cool." She met Sam's gaze.

His breath came out in a frosty stream, and

his black hair blew around in the afternoon breeze. His eyes were even bluer than the sky.

"Have you moved in yet?" she asked.

"I checked out of the hotel, if that's what you mean. My duffel bag is still in the truck. I wanted to talk to you first."

Kyle looked up at Sam anxiously. "You're going to stay here, aren't you, Sam? Grandpa Ed said you were going to stay until after Christmas."

"I haven't made up my mind yet, Kyle."

"But you *have* to stay." Kyle wiped his nose with the back of his mitten. "Hawk's Roost is really cool. And if you stay until the lake melts, then we can go boating and fishing and swimming. We can dive off the dock."

Kyle's words made Melanie realize she had a lot more to worry about than just her bruised heart. Her son had been getting progressively closer to Sam. But because of his job, Sam could be gone at a moment's notice and for long periods of time.

The last thing Kyle needed was another absentee hero.

It would break Kyle's heart when Sam left. She knew she ought to prepare him for that moment, and she might as well start now.

Only Sam beat her to it.

"Whoa!" Sam cupped Kyle's chin. "Christmas

here sounds wonderful, champ, but summer's a long way off. And before I bring my gear in, I'd like to talk to your mother about a couple of things first. Okay with you?"

"Okay, Sam."

"You practice walking the puck back and forth with the stick. I'll be watching you from that bench over there."

"Sure."

Melanie walked over to one of the benches by the lake, while Sam skated beside her. Sam brushed the snow off, and they sat down.

"My son likes you a lot."

"I like him, too. He's a great kid." Sam took a deep breath. "Look, are you sure you don't have a problem with me staying here? Yesterday you didn't look happy."

Melanie shook her head. "It's okay. I had planned on celebrating Christmas here with Kyle instead of at home. Memories, you know."

"Then I'll go back to the Pine Tree Motel."

She shook her head. "Not a chance. I'll bet my pay on the Phaeton that your room is already taken. The snowmobile races start tomorrow. People are pouring into Hawk's Lake."

"But there's probably another room nearby."

She smiled. "Maybe over in Vermont, but not in these mountains."

"I'd go to Cal Lippert's, but his in-laws are visiting," he said.

"Sam, don't worry about it, please. It's fine." She was surprised that she really meant it.

"If you're sure...." Sam thought for a minute. "Why can't we all stay here together? It looks like this place has about fifteen rooms."

"Us? Stay together? That wouldn't be a good idea." She wondered why her stomach was jumping at the thought. "Kyle loves playing hockey with you, and he would be heartbroken if you left, so you move in and enjoy the place."

Maybe she'd be heartbroken if he left, too.

"Thanks." He nodded. "You know, Hawk's Lake makes me so homesick. I wish my folks had let me know they were selling the farm. I would have bought it."

"You didn't know?"

"I was in India, and they couldn't get in touch with me. By the time I got the message and got back to them, it had been sold. Funny, I always thought the place would be there to come home to."

"I'm so sorry," Melanie said. She couldn't imagine her father selling the garage or Hawk's Roost and not telling her. She touched his arm.

He shrugged. "Really, it's no big deal."

"It *is* a big deal. It meant a lot to you." They sat together in silence for a moment.

"Sam... How come you're not working as a manager for emergency relief anymore?"

There was a long silence. Then he took a breath and lowered his voice. "I felt that I couldn't perform the job properly after your husband's death."

Melanie could hear the light swish of Kyle's skates on the lake, and the heavier sound of Sam's breathing.

He looked over at Kyle. "I don't want to jeopardize any more lives because of my indecision."

She pulled on his arm to turn him toward her. "Sam, after our talk yesterday, I hope you don't feel that way anymore." She looked into his eyes. "People need your skills."

He gave a slight smile, but his eyes didn't lose their haunted look. "That's nice of you to say."

"So, it's settled? You'll stay at Hawk's Roost and join us for Christmas?"

"Yes. Thanks. I'd love to," he said.

"I have to warn you that on Christmas Day, my father invites half the village over."

"Sounds like fun."

"If you don't mind, would you watch Kyle for a

little longer?" Melanie stood. "I'll make us some lunch. Probably only canned soup until one of us goes shopping, but I'll give a yell when it's ready."

"Okay."

While walking to the cottage, she wondered if Sam was lonely. Her father had picked up on it, but she'd been too busy being angry to notice.

Melanie let herself into the big house, kicked off her boots on the braided rug by the front door and headed to the thermostat to turn up the heat in the great room.

She headed for the walk-in fireplace made of huge river rock and started a fire to supplement the furnace.

Going to the kitchen, she searched the pantry for cans of soup. She took out two cans of chicken noodle and two of chili. There was nothing worse than chili in a can, but Kyle loved it. She hoped Sam would, too.

She got everything ready and set it on the stove to heat, then filled the tea kettle and put it on to boil. Through the big kitchen window, she could see Sam and Kyle still playing hockey.

She could tell by the big grin on Kyle's face that he was having a wonderful time with Sam. Sam was at his side, demonstrating a move. Kyle smiled up at him and gave the puck a fast whack. They high-fived, and her heart warmed.

It was hard to resist a man who was so terrific with her son.

With lunch nearly ready, she went back into the great room and poked at the fire, moving the logs so they'd catch quickly. It was almost warm enough for her to take her coat off.

She stepped onto the porch and rang the big ship's bell.

Kyle's voice echoed across the frozen landscape. "That's the bell, Sam. When you hear the bell, you have to go up to the camp."

"Aye, skipper. Whatever you say," Sam answered.

They both waved to her, and she smiled and waved back. "Lunch is ready," she yelled.

Sam stopped at Jack's truck and took two pairs of boots from the floor of the backseat— a big pair and a small pair.

As they sat on the bottom step of the front porch, Sam helped Kyle off with his skates and into his boots.

Kyle didn't make a move to go inside, but sat watching and waiting until Sam was finished. Then they stood up in unison.

Yeah, Kyle was certainly infatuated with Sam. She hated to break the boy's heart by reminding him that Sam would be leaving when Christmas was over.

"Bring in your skates and put them on the rug so they can dry out," she instructed as they entered the cottage. "And hang your coats on the hooks in the mudroom."

"Okay, Mom."

Sam took off Kyle's ski cap and ruffled his hair. As Kyle led Sam into the mudroom, Kyle started to sing the French Christmas song that Sam had taught him. To his credit, he remembered every word.

"This is one magnificent place." Sam whistled as he ran his hand down a peeled beam and stared up at the big logs that held up the cathedral ceiling. "Outstanding." He warmed his hands by the fireplace, then turned to Melanie. "You could fit the entire Pine Tree Motel in here about eight times."

She chuckled and some of the tension she'd felt after their last conversation dissipated.

"I'll give you a tour later," she said. "You can pick out a bedroom and I'll make it up."

"I can take care of that."

She shook her head. "You're our guest."

An excited shiver went through her at the realization that Sam would be staying another week after the Snow Festival ended. What was she doing? She was starting to think like Kyle.

"You guys must be starved. Everything's ready in the kitchen."

Lunch was surprisingly fun. Kyle entertained them with stories about the power swing that he'd learned from Sam. Her son's sweet little face was glowing.

"Is Sam going to stay here, Mom? Huh?" Kyle asked.

She put her spoon down. "Yes." She looked at Sam. "And he's going to stay for Christmas."

When Kyle hooted loudly and squirmed in his chair, Melanie steadied his chili bowl as Sam picked up his mug of hot cocoa.

Melanie studied Sam across the table. He looked so hot, he took her breath away. When he looked back at her, she felt all boneless and jittery. She hadn't felt like that in several years. Remembering their kisses, she couldn't concentrate on even the simple task of eating her soup.

"Are we going to stay here, too, Mom?" Kyle asked, breaking into her thoughts.

She stiffened, wondering what to say. She didn't want Kyle to think that the three of them were going to become one happy family. Even though a tiny part of her was beginning to wonder what that would be like...

"Let's leave Sam alone. We'll stay overnight

on Christmas Eve with your uncles and grandpa like we always do," she said.

"Cool," Kyle said, appeased.

"Grandpa Ed and Uncle Brian and Uncle Jack make a big breakfast on Christmas Day. They said that this year, I'm big enough to help. You can help, too, Sam."

"I'd be happy to. Sounds like fun."

Melanie turned toward Kyle. "If you guys aren't tired from all that hockey, I think we ought to put on snow shoes and cut down two Christmas trees today. One for Hawk's Roost and one for Sunshine Cottage."

"Cool." Kyle took another spoonful of chili.

"I can't think of anything I'd rather do." Sam smiled at Melanie. "Or two other people I'd rather be with."

Melanie couldn't believe she'd just invited Sam to cut their trees. But she could hardly walk away with Kyle and leave Sam alone. That wouldn't be polite.

Who was she kidding? She wanted Sam to join them. When had she started to enjoy his company? She wasn't even sure. All she knew was that she needed to stop thinking of him, needed to stop inviting him to do things.

And that was just what she was going to do—starting right after the tree expedition.

Chapter Eleven

They slipped into snowshoes and tramped through the woods around Hawk's Roost to find two perfect Christmas trees. After a while, Kyle grew tired and hitched a ride on the toboggan that Sam pulled, content to drag the tips of his gloves through the snow.

Melanie pointed to a Douglas fir on a slight incline. It looked like the perfect tree. "How about that one over there for Sunshine Cottage?"

"That little one?" Kyle shook his head. "Nah."

"It'll look much bigger in our living room, sweetie."

"Okay. Can I cut it?" Kyle asked. The size of

the tree was quickly forgotten for the chance to play with manly tools.

Melanie reached for the bow saw that lay in the back of her sled. "You can help, but I'll do the sawing."

Sam held out a hand to take the saw from her. "Would you let me do the honors?"

"That's not necessary. I can do it."

"I know you can," Sam said. "But you have to be careful with trees. If it falls the wrong way, someone could get hurt."

He took a deep breath and raised his eyes to the sky. "I'm sorry," Sam said.

Melanie hadn't followed his train of thought at first, but then she realized what he was apologizing for—he'd been thinking about Mike.

"And I just wanted us to have a good day," he mumbled.

"We *are* having a good day, Sam." She turned to Kyle. "Sweetie, I think the tree is straight, but will you check it carefully from all angles?"

"Sure, Mom," he said eager to help.

She helped him up from the toboggan, and he snowshoed up the hill. As she watched him, she thought about inviting Sam back to Sunshine Cottage—maybe cooking dinner for him. She didn't want him to be alone at The Roost with nothing to do but wait until he had to appear at one of the Snow Festival events. That wouldn't be very hospitable of her, would it?

Hospitality...right.

In spite of Melanie's resolve not to do any more inviting, she gripped Sam's arm before she could change her mind. "Sam...would you come to dinner at my place? It would just be the two of us."

Just the two of us.

The words hung in the air, and for a long moment, all they could do was look at each other. Melanie told herself that the warm rush that coursed through her was healthy. She was a woman and he was a man—a sexy man.

But desire had nothing to do with it, she told herself. Really, she was just trying to make things up to him. Or so she was trying to convince herself.

Melanie found her voice first. "How about tomorrow night at Sunshine Cottage—unless you have to preside over the snowmobile races? I'll ask my father to take Kyle overnight." She lowered her eyes. "This will give us a chance to get to know each other better."

"I'll let Cal know that I can't make the races. From what I remember of the schedule, I was just supposed to award the prizes to the win-

ners. I'm sure he'd love to do it." He winked.
"I'll just say that I got a better offer."

Even in the twenty-degree weather, she felt
hot enough to melt.

Just the two of us, Sam repeated in his mind
as he sawed the tree for Sunshine Cottage.

He didn't know why Melanie had lowered her
guard and invited him to dinner, but whatever
the reason, he was excited at the idea. Somehow,
he'd have to keep his desire for her under control. He'd never felt drawn to any woman as he
did to her. He liked her strength, her stoicism.

And yet, she was a passionate woman. He
knew that from the way she responded to his
kisses.

He shook his head. Right now, he'd better
keep his mind on sawing the tree! "Kyle, are
you ready?"

The boy nodded seriously.

"Watch your face so you don't get scratched
by the needles and reach in and grab the trunk.
It's going to fall over there." He pointed to the
left. "When I tell you to let go, let go really fast
and take a couple of steps back. Got it?"

"Got it," Kyle said.

"Anything you want me to do?" Melanie
asked.

"We men have things under control. Right, Kyle?"

"Right!"

"Okay. Hold on now, Kyle." Sam made a few more sweeps with the saw, and held on to the trunk himself so the tree wouldn't kick. "Remember, when I say let go, *let go* and take two quick steps back."

He could see the concentration on the boy's face.

"Let go!" Sam yelled.

Sam gave the tree an extra push away from the boy. Kyle did as instructed, and the tree fell right where Sam had predicted.

Melanie hugged Kyle. "It'll be beautiful in our living room, sweetie."

"Yeah! Now let's cut down a really big one for Sam."

"Kyle, you mean a tree for Hawk's Roost," Melanie corrected. "A tree for *everyone* to enjoy."

"That's what I said." Kyle looked at her as if she had suddenly sprouted another head.

Sam wondered why Melanie was stressing that it wasn't just his tree. Surely Kyle knew that. "We have to tie this tree up first and put it on the sled before we get another. We'll pick it up on the way back."

Kyle was instantly at Sam's side, happy to assist him. He helped Sam wrap the rope around the branches and tie it off, and the three of them rolled it onto the toboggan.

"I see a perfect tree for Sam." Kyle pointed to a huge blue spruce towering fifty feet in the air. It was loaded with big pinecones and long needles.

Sam put his hands on his hips and chuckled. "Now, Kyle, do I look like I could cut that huge tree with this little saw?"

"My father was cutting a tree," Kyle said. "But then it fell over. It was a big tree like that, I guess."

Sam met Melanie's gaze.

"Kyle…um…your dad…" Melanie's mouth moved, but no more words came out.

"The tree fell into the river," Kyle stated flatly. "My dad fell into the river, too."

Melanie cleared her throat. "Kyle, Sam was there that night. He knows what happened to your dad."

"You were there?"

It seemed that Kyle didn't know all the details about the accident. Sam raised an eyebrow at Melanie, and she nodded slightly. He took that to mean that she trusted him with her son, and gave him permission to explain some things to Kyle.

"I tried to help your father, Kyle. I tried to get him out of the water, but it was dark and I couldn't find him."

Tears began to form in the little boy's eyes, and Sam knelt on one knee before him. He'd been so busy being wrapped up in his conflicted feelings for Melanie that he'd almost forgotten about Kyle's pain.

"But my dad could swim. Why didn't he swim, Sam?"

Sam looked up at Melanie with another silent question. She nodded again, her face as white as the snow around her.

Sam prayed he could answer Kyle's question without making things worse. Just looking at this little boy's face with his drippy nose, his rosy cheeks and his hair sticking out from under his ski cap, made Sam want to crush the boy to him and never let him go.

He took Kyle's mittened hands instead. "Kyle, the water was very, very cold and it was running fast. Your dad tried to swim, he really did. He fought hard. I pushed him toward the bank of the river, but he got really tired from the cold water."

Well, that was mostly the truth.

Kyle sucked some snow off his mittens. "Grandpa Ed said that we should be glad that you were here during the storm. It's cuz you help people when there's a dis...dis..."

"Disaster," Sam supplied.

Kyle's face was serious. "I think you're a hero, too."

Sam brushed off the snow that was accumulating on the boy's parka. "I think that a hero is someone who shows great courage. Your father was a hero. He had great courage to climb that icy, broken tree to cut it so it wouldn't fall on the switching station. You and your mother are heroes for going on without your father."

Kyle hurled himself at Sam and gave him a big hug around the neck.

"Thanks for trying to save my father," Kyle whispered in his ear. "I still think you're a hero."

Out of the corner of his eye, Sam could see Melanie walk behind a cluster of hemlocks. He could hear her crying softly. Sam closed his eyes, hugged Kyle tightly and just let him cry for his father.

A gentle snow started to fall. The forest was silent, except for the tears of a woman and boy Sam knew he'd already fallen for.

* * *

Later, as they cut down another tree for Hawk's Roost, Melanie couldn't help but reflect on how gently Sam talked to Kyle. He was so caring with her son, understanding and loving. And when Kyle walked into Sam's arms, Melanie's heart melted.

She told herself that it always melted when a big, strong man comforted a young child, but there was more to it than that. When Sam wrapped Kyle in his arms, he seemed to actually want to take Kyle's pain away and absorb it himself. She knew that Sam would make a great father.

She'd always thought that Mike was a good father. When Mike was home, he'd paid attention to Kyle—or maybe that was just because Kyle spent hours sitting next to his father on the couch as he watched tapes of games. Kyle would stick to Mike like pinesap because he'd missed him.

And then Mike would leave again for another scouting trip.

Just like Sam would leave after Christmas.

Sam lugged the heavy tree stand out of the attic and set it in the middle of the floor-to-ceiling window to the right of the fireplace.

Kyle and Sam hung the lights on the tree and sang the French Christmas carol that Sam had taught him. Then he taught them both another one. Melanie and Kyle sang along as they all hung the ornaments that had been in her family for decades.

"What about the angel, Mom?"

"Coming up." She went over to the special box, the original box that she and her mother had saved throughout the years and pulled out the old ornament, straightening the angel's outfit.

Sam peered over her shoulder. "That's a beautiful angel. A family heirloom?"

Melanie could barely nod as he leaned over her and touched the dress of the angel. His other hand gripped her waist, and she could feel the warmth of his body behind her and the whisper of his breath against her neck. She closed her eyes, enjoying the feel of him, the closeness, the smell of the outdoors that lingered on his clothes and mixed with the scent of the freshly cut tree. She fought against the thought of leaning her head back against his broad chest, and just enjoyed the moment.

"My great-grandma Sophie crocheted the dress," she finally said. "The doll she used was one that her mother had as a child. I loved this angel growing up and couldn't wait to see it every year."

He moved back, leaving her swaying on her feet.

"Why don't you take the angel for your tree, at your house," he said. His voice was deep and low.

"No way," Kyle said. "That angel has always been here. On the Hawk's Roost tree."

"That's true," Melanie said.

"Okay." He turned to Kyle. "What's her name? The name of our angel on our tree in Canada was Angelique."

Melanie stared down at the porcelain, painted face. "We've always just called her the Christmas angel."

"Sam, how do you say Christmas angel in French?" Kyle asked.

"Ange de Noël."

"Cool. Then let's call her Angie day no elle," Kyle said.

Melanie chuckled. "Okay."

Sam pulled over the stepladder. "Melanie, I think you should do the honors and put Angie on the tree."

Sam steadied the ladder as she climbed it. When she was on the third rung from the top, she felt Sam's hands on her buttocks, then the back of her legs, holding her steady.

Even through her sturdy jeans, she could feel each of his fingers on her. She could imagine him behind her, looking up, his blue eyes twinkling in merriment when he realized how his touch was affecting her. And she was so obvious about her reaction to him. How could he miss it?

She took her time in moving lights and ornaments to pick out a good safe place for Angie to stand, telling herself that she was just trying to make sure the angel was straight.

She was glad Kyle was on the far side of the tree, so he couldn't see what Sam's hands were doing.

The ribbon of the angel's waistband was supposed to tie her to the tree, but Melanie's fumbling fingers wouldn't work, not when Sam was getting her all flushed and distracted.

She swayed on the ladder as she reached for the ribbon that had slipped through her fingers. His hands cupped her buttocks, and a half moan, half gasp escaped her lips.

"Sorry, but I don't want you to fall. We'd have to do all our beautiful work over again." His voice was low, husky.

She laughed. "Gee, thanks."

With a fingertip, she caught the other ribbon. Leaning over as far as she could, she tried to tie a bow. She just needed another inch...

She was going to fall into the tree. She jerked herself back, but overcorrected. She felt herself flying through the air, arms flailing.

"Oh!"

But when she landed, she didn't hear a dull thud as she had before. And when she opened her eyes, everything was bright and clear.

Sam had caught her. Her arms were around his neck and her cheek was buried in his fisherman's knit sweater. He was smiling down at her.

"Just like an angel falling from the sky. *Ange de Noël.*"

His arms were strong behind her back and knees. The skin on his neck was tanned. His jaw couldn't have been more chiseled if a sculptor had created it.

Finally, she got her mind and mouth working at the same time. "Thank you."

He tipped her and set her back on her feet. She still swayed a little.

He held on to her. "My pleasure."

Something crackled between them, hot and intense and sensual. Thinking that she'd been cooler with just her T-shirt, she slipped off her sweatshirt just as she noticed that Sam was shedding his sweater, too. He wore a striped golf shirt underneath.

She saw Kyle staring at them. That was just what she didn't need—Kyle thinking that something was going on between the two of them, or that Sam would be staying in Hawk's Lake forever.

Melanie couldn't catch her breath for a second. "I was just stunned when I fell, honey. Sam caught me. It kind of shook me up."

He shrugged. "Okay."

Things were so simple in Kyle's world.

She tucked her hair behind her ear. "How about if you guys get the boxes packed up and back to the attic? In the meantime, I'll fix up a bedroom for Sam."

"I'll ask Grandpa Ed if you can stay as long as you want. Okay, Sam? We can go swimming and boating and—"

Sam looked at Melanie.

"Kyle, Sam has a job. Remember how he helped us out last year? He might have another area to help or even another country. He could get a call at any time and then have to fly right out of here." She looked at Sam. "Right, Sam?"

He met her eyes and simply nodded. She could tell he didn't want to leave, either.

Heaven help her, she wanted him to stay. Hopefully, everything would be calm at Christmas, and there wouldn't be a disaster somewhere.

"Right," Sam echoed.

Melanie got up to get the bed linens for the big king bedroom behind the great room to make up a room for Sam, but she still could hear Sam talking to Kyle.

"My family is getting together after Christmas because my mother and father are traveling. We live all over, but we all try to get together whenever we can."

"I wouldn't like it if my uncles or my grandpa lived someplace else. I like them here," Kyle said. "But my dad was never here. I was mad at him all the time because he wasn't," Kyle continued softly. "But if he was still here, I wouldn't be mad at him anymore for always being away and never calling me."

Melanie gasped. She'd never realized that Kyle had been that affected by Mike's absences.

"I'm away a lot, too, Kyle. It's my job, just like it was your dad's job."

"Do you like to be away a lot, Sam?"

"No, but I have to go where I'm needed."

Sam nicely turned their conversation to hockey,

and Melanie returned, with a heavier heart, to making Sam's bed.

Even if she was willing to trust a man again, there could be no future with Sam—for Kyle's sake, too.

Melanie sighed as she covered the pillows with cases. She knew that Sam would like the first-floor bedroom that overlooked pines on one side and the lake on the other. It had its own little deck.

It was her room whenever she stayed at Hawk's Roost, but this year, she'd stay upstairs to be near Kyle. Both rooms had their own fireplaces and full bathrooms, but what she liked about this room was that it caught the morning sun. She loved sitting out on the deck, having her morning coffee and watching the light shimmering on the lake.

She shook out a flat sheet with sailboats on it and hummed the new Christmas carol that Sam had just taught them as she made up his bed.

All too easily, Melanie could picture him lying on the bed naked, his body muscled, tanned and hard. His blue eyes would beckon her to join him. He'd hold out his hand and gently pull her onto the bed....

Dust, she told herself firmly, cheeks flaming with heat. She should dust the room.

She rarely dusted, but she had to do something. She needed to stop thinking about Sam as a lover. Maybe it was because she hadn't had sex in a long time.

But sex with Sam LeDoux? Not too long ago, she was blaming him for everything from the humidity in summer to the snow in winter. Now he was starring in her fantasies.

She went to the kitchen and got some paper towels and a can of furniture polish.

Sam and Kyle were chatting away. The two of them were sweeping the great room, cleaning up the pine needles. They were good for each other, that much was obvious.

She hoped that someday he'd have children of his own. He was that type of man—a family man. But she'd thought that Mike was, too. Maybe she just wasn't a good judge of character.

By the time she'd finished dusting and went out to the living room, Sam and Kyle were fast asleep on the couch. Kyle's legs were stretched out on top of Sam's.

If she didn't know better, she'd say they looked like father and son.

Melanie yawned. There was nothing like a tramp through the snow in the crisp, cold mountain air to tire everyone out.

She went to the linen closet and took out three blankets. She put one over Sam and then Kyle. Then she took another and curled up on the other sofa.

She was content to listen to their steady breathing until the rhythm lulled her into sleep.

Sam awoke to find Melanie dozing on the other sofa. She opened her eyes slowly when she heard him move. Glancing at Kyle, he gently moved the boy's legs off his, got up and held his hand out to her.

With a questioning look, she took his hand, and he pulled her to her feet. Then he picked her up off the floor and carried her to the room where she'd just made the bed. He laid her down gently.

"Sam, maybe I shouldn't...*we* shouldn't."

"Maybe not, but it feels right, doesn't it?"

She nodded. "It does."

"Do you want me to stop?"

"No."

He knew damn well there were still unresolved issues between them. Maybe they never would be resolved. But at this moment, he just wanted to be with her, wanted to feel her body next to his.

Without a sound, he took off her shoes, then

kicked off his own. Lying down beside her, he brushed the hair off her face. Her skin felt so warm, so smooth. Her hand went to his arm, but she didn't push him away, just looked at him, a hint of hesitation in her eyes. Then she smiled slightly. He took that as an invitation, and bent his head and tasted her lips. They were sweet and inviting, and he wanted more. He pulled her closer to him, trying to take it slow, but with Melanie, he found himself as crazy as a teen. He kissed her again and again, and when she made a slight sound of pleasure, his kisses became harder and she matched his fervor.

She pulled him over to lie across her, and he searched for the edge of her top. His hand urgently sought her breasts, but a noise from the great room stopped him cold.

"Kyle," she whispered, panic in her eyes. Jumping off the bed, she pulled down her sweater, fixed her hair and gave him what he thought was a regretful glance before she hurried out of the room.

Sam got up and smoothed the bed linens. Then he found a bathroom and splashed some cold water on his face, thinking that he should take a cold shower instead.

How could he be so darn stupid? It was a bad idea to start something with Melanie. He was getting too caught up in the whole family thing—playing hockey with Kyle, hiking in the woods with the two of them, decorating a tree. But this wasn't his house, Kyle wasn't his son and Melanie wasn't his wife.

With his job, it was impossible for him to settle down and establish a relationship with anyone. And he loved what he did. He was needed and his expertise was invaluable—that's what the higher ups always told him, and inside himself Sam knew this was true.

But the last thing Kyle needed was another absentee father.

After these three weeks as grand marshal were over and he was convinced that Melanie and Kyle were okay, he figured he'd be ready to get back to work.

He couldn't stay in this picture-perfect town. And he couldn't let himself fall for Melanie. He had a responsibility to do his job and do it well.

Besides, Melanie certainly didn't need another neglectful husband. He would just have to try and keep his distance from her.

For all of them.

Chapter Twelve

Sam opened the wine he'd brought as Melanie set out two glasses. After he poured, he looked around the kitchen for something that might give a hint as to what she was cooking for dinner.

"I smell garlic, but I don't see anything," he said.

"I might as well confess that I can't cook."

"Your brother Brian warned me about your cooking, and he gave me these." He held up a roll of antacids.

She chuckled and shook her head. "You're safe. I got takeout from Momma Luigi's. Spaghetti and meatballs. It's warming in the oven."

"Anyone who can restore cars like you can't be expected to cook, too."

"Flattery will get you everywhere." Melanie took her wineglass and held it up. "What shall we toast to?" she asked.

"New beginnings," Sam said, feeling that was an appropriate toast for the two of them.

"To new beginnings," Melanie smiled, as they clinked glasses.

He pulled out a kitchen chair for her. He smelled the delicate scent of gardenias that he'd always associated with her. She wore a red satin blouse that accented her breasts and a pair of dark jeans that showed her curves. A silvery belt looped around her slim waist. She had on a pair of red socks with candy canes all over them and no shoes.

She was beautiful.

He took a seat opposite her and poured her some wine.

They clinked their glasses.

Melanie's eyes met his. "I'm glad you came to dinner, Sam."

"I've been wondering why you invited me."

She sighed. "Oh, I don't know. I guess I wanted to make up for treating you so miserably when you first came to town, and I didn't want you to be at The Roost all alone."

"You didn't know everything."

She shook her head in disagreement. "Even so, I shouldn't have blamed you."

"I blamed myself, so you were in good company."

She smiled slightly. "Well, let's leave all that behind us. I invited you for supper, and supper it shall be. Everything is hot. The garlic bread is in the oven. The table is set in the dining room." Her eyes surveyed the kitchen. "And nothing is on fire. I declare the meal a success already."

Sam remembered their evening at Momma Luigi's. It was amazing how things had progressed so quickly since then. In fact, he knew that if Kyle hadn't been at the cottage yesterday, he would have made love to her. And judging from her eager response to his kisses, she would have been a willing partner.

And Melanie had invited him to dinner, and Kyle wasn't at home. Was he reading something into that?

They brought everything to the dining room and ate by the light of two red tapers and the glow of the Christmas tree in the living room.

"This is romantic," he said, "And you look especially beautiful tonight."

"Thank you," she said, seeming pleased.

They talked about their favorite Christmas

memories, and then Melanie asked, "What would be your perfect Christmas gift?"

"Hmm…" He thought for a while. How could he tell her that he was already getting the perfect gift by spending Christmas with her and Kyle? "I'd like to know for sure that I won't get a call—that there won't be any disasters in the world."

He could tell by the happy smile on her face that she liked the idea, too.

"How about you, Melanie? If you could have anything in the world, what would you want?"

"Oh, I don't know. I have most everything I want," she said. "I have my memory back. Kyle and my family are all in good health." She didn't quite meet his eyes.

"Cheater," Sam accused. "What do you really want?"

She crossed her arms and laughed. "Okay. No comment."

She wasn't parting with any information, that was for sure. He stood. "Let me clean this up."

"Don't you dare. You're my guest." She got up with her plate in hand. "Go relax by the Christmas tree. I won't be long."

"Okay."

Sam put another log on the fire and poked around a little so it wouldn't die out. Taking a seat on the comfortable flowered couch, he studied the room.

He liked this room as much as the kitchen. The whole downstairs, with its big windows, hardwood floors and tall ceilings, was cozy and comfortable and big enough that a good half-dozen kids could play in it.

It was a house for a big family.

Melanie returned carrying two glasses of wine in her hands. She handed one to him and sat down on the far end of the couch. She took a sip then faced him.

"You know, it's snowing hard out there. I'm getting a little worried about everyone at the snowmobile races," she said. "How can something so beautiful be so treacherous at the same time?"

He looked out the front window. She was right. It was almost a whiteout. "There's a lot of people in town for the races. Driving conditions are going to be more dangerous than usual, especially for people who aren't used to these roads."

"Maybe you should stay here overnight instead of driving back to The Roost," she said, her eyes meeting his.

He couldn't talk if he'd wanted to—he wasn't sure how to respond. Was this the invitation he'd been fantasizing about?

"Sam?" Her voice was barely a whisper.

Unable to hold back anymore, he reached for her and pulled her into his arms. She didn't protest, so he kissed her gently. Still no protest.

Her hands went to his chest, and he could feel their warmth through his shirt. She didn't push him away, but clenched the material in her hands and pulled him even closer.

"Melanie?" he asked, searching her face for an answer.

She gave a slight nod and a knowing smile. That was all the permission he needed.

He dispensed with his shirt, then her blouse. Her pink bra was all lace. Sam made quick work of the clasp and brushed the fabric aside. Her breasts were as perfect as he'd imagined— a perfect fit for his hands.

He tossed an afghan on the floor and pulled her to the plush carpet. By the glow of the Christmas tree, he tasted her nipples, moved his hand to her heat, and she spread her legs to give him more access.

"I want you, Sam," she whispered. "I do."

He quickly removed the rest of her clothing until she lay naked before him, the lights of the tree making her look almost ethereal.

"My angel," he said.

He unzipped his pants with one hand and

pulled his wallet out of his pocket with the other, dumping the contents on the floor. Looking through the mess, he found what he was looking for—a condom.

He kicked his underwear and pants off, and put the condom where he could reach it. He felt as clumsy as a high-school kid, and less debonair.

They had all night, and he wanted to take it slow. He wanted to kiss and caress every inch of Melanie's scented skin.

Starting with her lips, he made his way down her neck and back to her breasts. His hand found her center, and he heard her gasp when his fingers parted her.

"It's been a long time, Sam."

"I'll make it as good as I can for you, Melanie."

Her green eyes pooled with tears, but there was a smile on her face.

He covered her mouth with his. He traced her lips with his tongue, and she opened for him. Their tongues engaged in an erotic dance while his thumb teased her little nub of skin below as she cried out.

He opened the condom wrapper with his teeth, and when he was done, she pulled him over her.

Desire blurred her thinking, pulsed through

her veins—she couldn't stop herself if she tried. She wanted him, and she was going to give him her body. Just once. The need to feel him inside her was blocking her common sense.

She liked his weight on her. He felt good. He smelled good. His body was strong and lean, all muscle and sinew. When he whispered in French, she was ready to swoon.

"Please, tell me what you said." She reached for him, stroking him. He was hard and ready, and she wanted him.

"I said that I want to take it slow, but I can't. And if you don't stop moving your hands, or if I don't get inside you soon, I'm going to embarrass myself." He kissed the tip of her nose and smiled.

Melanie returned his smile, reveling in the fact that he found her exciting. Years of disinterest from Mike had made her feel undesirable. With Sam, she felt wanted and sexy.

She gripped him gently and guided him to her core. "Now, Sam. I want you."

He entered gently, slowly, but that wasn't enough. With an impatient thrust of her hips, she took him deeper.

She could see sweat on his upper lip. He was trying to hold back for her.

"Sam?"

"You feel so good."

"More."

With a slow movement of his hips, he filled her completely. The pace increased, and Melanie met him thrust for thrust. She tightened around him and heard him groan. She felt like she was soaring and never wanted to come back to earth.

Sam shuddered in release, and when he smiled at Melanie, she was blinking back tears.

Their bodies were still joined. She loved that feeling, and didn't want him to move. She pulled him down for a kiss.

She'd been falling in love with him all along. It had happened so slowly that she couldn't exactly pinpoint when she started to soften toward him.

But she couldn't be falling for him. Not him. Not any man. Not again.

When he moved off her, she felt cold, even though the fireplace was generating more than enough heat.

She pulled the afghan over them, and the slight breeze made several of the ornaments on the tree tinkle in sweet tones. He gathered her close to his side and for a long time, they were silent, content simply to look at the sparkling tree and to be with each other.

Over the crackling of the fireplace, Melanie heard rapid tapping on the windows and what sounded like nails pummeling the roof.

Hailstones.

Sam heard it, too. He raised his eyes to the ceiling. "It's too early for Santa Claus."

A sickening dread settled in her gut. Instinctively, Melanie knew what was happening.

Then the town's siren went off.

"There's an emergency," Melanie said. Her voice was quiet, raspy. She stared at the Christmas tree. "Not again."

Sam felt the familiar adrenaline rush, and automatically scrambled for his clothes, shrugging into them as fast as he could.

He moved the curtains on the front window and looked out. "Hail. Mixed with snow." He gave a long whistle. "And it's very windy. It looks bad."

Melanie looked up at him from the floor. "Don't go," she said. Her face had lost all color.

Sam helped her up and wrapped the afghan tighter around her. He hugged her close to him. Now he knew her secrets, what had happened that night, why there was an edge of panic in her voice.

She clung to him. "Maybe it's a fire or a water

break or something. They don't need you for that."

His cell phone went off. He gave a quick glance at the number and answered it.

"Cal, what's up? Of course I'll help. I'll be right there. Won't take me long. Yeah, I remember how to get there." He closed the cover on his phone, and met Melanie's frightened eyes.

"It's just like that night."

He took her hands in his. "Melanie, please don't worry. I do this for a living. And I'm not Mike."

"This isn't about Mike. This is about you. Sam, I really care about you."

He was speechless for a moment. To hear her say those words aloud gave a lift to his heart.

"Don't look so astonished." She put her hands on her hips. "I don't just make love under the Christmas tree on the living room floor with every Canuck who comes to town."

He grinned. "That's good, since I was thinking of arranging an exhibition hockey game with the Canucks next year for the Snow Festival."

She couldn't help but laugh. He was good for her.

"This is my job, Melanie."

She nodded, her eyes glassy.

"You have to trust me." He kissed her as his cell rang again. He checked the number. "I've got to go. It's the transformer station again." He shook his head. "I thought the town was going to clear all those trees from around it last spring."

"There were a lot of protesters—conservationists—who were against it, and Cal didn't want them sitting in the trees."

"Cal is a consummate politician."

Sam moved away from Melanie, sat down on a bench by the front door, and stepped into his boots. He had severe-weather gear in the truck that he could put on at the site.

"Cal said that they cut the snowmobile races short and sent everyone home, so don't worry about Kyle or your brothers."

"Good." She had just been wondering about that. "Take care of yourself, Sam."

"I will, and you stay warm, Melanie. If the power goes out here, keep the fire going."

She rolled her eyes. "I've lived in these mountains all my life."

He slanted his head and grinned. "I know, but it makes me feel better to say it."

She chuckled.

"I'll call you when I get a chance," Sam said.

Just then, the lights flickered and went out.

"Damn," he said.

As if she didn't hear, she sat down on the couch by the fire and wrapped the afghan tighter around her. He could see her shivering, probably more from fear than the cold. Her entire family—brothers, uncles and cousins—would answer the siren, except for her father, who would be watching Kyle.

"I'll come as soon as I can and help out at the shelter—that's the high school," she said, calmly. "And I'll bring thermos jugs of coffee to the site."

He shook his head. "You don't have to do that, Melanie. Stay home in case this gets worse. I don't want to scare you, but Cal said the National Weather Center just came out with a bulletin saying this surprise storm is expected to be worse than last year. So stay home. I don't want to worry about you."

"Looks like we're both worriers, huh?"

He tried to open her front door, but it was stuck. After throwing his shoulder against it, he was able to get it open. Ice coated the door. Ice coated his car and the sidewalk and the trees, which were bent over from the weight. If he didn't know how dangerous it was, he would have been awed by the fairyland effect.

He glanced back at Melanie. "I'll be back."

She nodded and gave a slight wave. He noticed a sad smile on her face.

No one had ever cared for him that much. No one had ever really worried about him. He wanted to kiss her again, hold her to him, but he knew he'd never be able to leave her if he did.

He shut the door and carefully picked his way down the stairs to the sidewalk, then started the truck and turned the heater and defroster on full blast. Grabbing his scraper, he went back outside and worked on clearing the ice off his windows so he could see to drive.

Before he pulled out of her driveway, he could see a shadow in the window—Melanie, pacing in front of her Christmas tree.

And he loved her for caring.

Still wrapped in the afghan that she'd shared with Sam, Melanie watched from her front window as the taillights of Jack's truck disappeared down the street.

She decided to call her father's house to talk to Kyle, who was usually a little scared when the power went out.

The phone was dead, so she found her cell phone and tried her father's cell phone, and then her brothers' cells. No connection.

Since the power was down, she got out her big

old blue enameled coffee pot. She filled the basket with coffee and set it on a hook over the fire. It'd be strong and hot—just the way the workers would like it.

Melanie took the stairs two at a time. She was going to get dressed and carefully drive out to the site. She'd been driving in these mountains for years, in all kinds of weather, and she knew what she was doing.

Almost a half hour later, she had loaded her car with water, hot coffee and blankets and was pulling out of the garage. She put it in four-wheel drive and tried to keep her teeth from rattling as she swayed and bounced over the icy ruts and drifts that had accumulated in the streets.

It was dark without the streetlights—she didn't dare drive faster than twenty miles an hour over the winding roads, slowing to a crawl when driving through drifts.

She drove past the high school—the designated refuge facility. The building had lights, courtesy of several huge generators, and a couple dozen vehicles were parked in the lot. With a tinge of guilt for not helping out there, Melanie kept driving to the transfer station.

A flagman motioned for her to pull over, so she came to a slippery stop. He was frosted with snow and wearing a ski mask and an orange-and-white fluorescent vest.

"Sorry, Mrs. Bennett, no one's allowed through here. Order of the sheriff."

She recognized the voice. Bobby Timmons. He worked as a mechanic at Hawk's Garage.

She checked the temperature on the gauge above her rearview mirror. "The volunteers need to keep warm, and I brought hot coffee. I also have blankets and a full tank of gas in case they want to warm up."

She handed Bobby a thermos of coffee, and he nodded his gratitude.

"Go ahead, but be careful."

"I will, Bobby."

Melanie fishtailed up the road, avoiding the fire trucks, cherry pickers and the portable lights shining at the station. Pulling into a clearing, she backed her Blazer in and cut the motor.

She wrapped a scarf around her face, tugged on another pair of mittens and walked carefully on the ice-covered path and tramped through drifts of crusty snow to where the crew was working, her arms full of thermos bottles.

Brushing off a snow-covered bench with a mitten, she set down all the refreshments.

She waited for a while, watching the workers move a particularly huge pine. Sam was shouting orders and gesturing to the crew. The men moved quickly and obeyed his every command, which was an achievement in itself. Her brother Jack was as stubborn and bossy as they came, and never listened to anyone unless he had the utmost respect for him. Brian was almost as bad as Jack, but Brian was usually smarter than anyone in command, and everyone knew it.

Melanie was happy to see that Sam had his confidence back.

After the tree was removed, Sam saw her standing there and whistled sharply for a break. "I see hot coffee, boys."

He was covered in snow, and his face was red from the cold. He took a red bandanna from his pocket and wiped his face.

In spite of the cold, Melanie felt her cheeks warm when she thought of their lovemaking under the Christmas tree.

He must have been thinking of the same thing. He gave her a wink and a big, sexy grin.

She grinned and waved, and pointed to the insulated containers. "Help yourselves, everyone," she shouted over the noise of the generators.

"I told you to stay home," Sam said. "And how did you get in here?" He wrapped his arm around her waist, a warm gesture that she was sure wasn't lost on her brothers.

"I bribed the flagman with coffee," she said.

"I'm glad you did," Sam said, pouring himself a cup.

Brian and Jack and the rest of the volunteers thanked her and moved toward the transfer station to look at the work still left to be done. She noticed her brothers talking together and glancing toward her. When she made eye contact with them, they quickly looked away.

They were always so overprotective.

As they walked through the snow, Sam filled her in on the latest word on the storm.

"There's some good news," he told her. "The latest from the National Weather Service is that the worst of the storm is going to miss us."

"That's definitely great news!"

"It's still going to snow—a lot—but it should stop by early afternoon. And we got some unexpected help from the owner of a lumberyard and several of his employees who were here for the snowmobile races. They've been invaluable in climbing and cutting."

"So everything is looking good?"

"Power should be restored in a couple of hours. I also convinced Cal that he needed to make an executive decision and get the lumberyard people to cut a big swath around this station so this won't happen again. In exchange, the lumberyard can have the trees, and the town can plant some new ones elsewhere."

"You're brilliant." Melanie grinned up at him.

"I'm glad you think so." He pulled her closer to him and pressed a warm kiss to her cold lips.

"I'll wait up for you."

"I don't know how long I'll be."

"That doesn't matter. I'll wait for you." Melanie had seen firsthand how good Sam was on the job, how he supervised the volunteers and how they respected him. If there were any doubts or shadows in her mind, she laid them to rest. Sam was good at what he did.

But that still didn't mean she wanted to open her heart to him entirely, or that she wanted to get seriously involved with another man. She reminded herself that his job took him away for long periods of time. And she wouldn't subject herself—or Kyle—to a situation like that again.

Chapter Thirteen

Sam opened the door to Sunshine Cottage as quietly as he could. It was three in the morning and the power had finally been restored.

He'd stopped at the refuge center, and everything was running smoothly. The handful of families who had relocated there would be transported home tomorrow afternoon, depending on the progress of the snowplows, which were working around the clock.

The little town of Hawk's Lake had learned a lot from last year, and was doing fine.

He felt like his old self again. No—like a new man. He was confident in his instructions and decisions again.

He felt as if that he could conquer anything that came his way. He was back and raring to go. And he owed it all to Melanie.

But at what expense? Melanie wasn't expecting him to stay—she'd made it clear she wasn't looking for a commitment.

But how did he feel about leaving her and Kyle?

Sam pulled off his boots and wet socks, and set them on a rubber mat. He hung his coat and clothes on various pegs on the wall to dry.

He walked into the living room in his boxers, and saw Melanie sleeping on the couch, wrapped in a red-and-green blanket—just like a Christmas present.

Her eyelashes fanned out on her cheeks like sable paintbrushes. Her eyelids were almost transparent, shell-like.

He had the urge to kiss her awake, but it was late…er, early.

The Christmas tree was on and glittering. The fire in the fireplace was out, so he built another.

He was way too comfortable in Melanie's house, in more ways than one. But he felt at home here in Sunshine Cottage and in this town that took him into their hearts—and vice versa.

On the coffee table, a coffee carafe and two

sandwiches sat on a silver tray, covered in plastic wrap to keep them fresh. Some pickles were on another dish beside it, also covered in plastic. A couple of paper Christmas napkins and a small bag of potato chips rounded out the tray.

He hadn't realized how hungry he actually was. As quietly as possible, he uncovered one of the sandwiches and started eating. When he finished, he settled back in the chair to sip his coffee and watch Melanie sleep. The blanket had slipped off her shoulder and he could see that her nightgown was almost transparent. He wondered if she'd chosen it just to torment him.

He thought about her distrust in their future together, and wondered if she trusted him never to lie to her. He wanted her enough to try and make it work, but how could he ease her fears and gain her trust?

And how would he earn a living? Disaster recovery was all he knew.

Melanie stirred, her eyes fluttering open. She smiled when she saw him.

"Good morning," he whispered. "Thanks for the sandwiches. I appreciate it."

"Mmm…hi, Sam." Her eyes were at half-mast. "What time is it?"

"Three-thirty-ish."

She stifled a yawn. "Let's go to bed."

He unplugged the Christmas tree, banked the fire, and then scooped a sleepy Melanie off the couch and into his arms. "Upstairs?" he asked.

"Guest room. Down the hall."

He carried her down the hall, enjoying the way she looked at him out of sleepy eyes.

"We'll sleep here," she said. "I don't want to be with you upstairs in the bed that…that I…"

"That you slept in with Mike."

"This room is…fresh," she said. "There aren't any regrets in here. Know what I mean?"

"Yes."

She pulled back the covers and plumped up the pillows. "The bathroom is down the hall. There's a little basket of toiletries that I keep for guests. Help yourself."

"Thanks."

He took a quick shower, brushed his teeth and returned to the guest room wrapped in a towel. It was dark except for a nightlight in the shape of a miniature Tiffany lamp on the far wall.

He dispensed with the towel, and climbed into bed. It felt good to stretch out next to her. Melanie's arm went around him, and he turned toward her, pulling her to him. She, too, was naked. He smiled, then kissed her.

"You're not too tired?" he asked.

Her palms traveled down his chest, settled on his nipples. "I've been waiting for you."

Her hands moved lower, tracing a path to his arousal. As their tongues moved in an exotic rhythm, she fondled him, massaged him, until he grew hard and thick.

He steadied her hands. "Stop." He barely breathed the words. He wanted her now. "My wallet?"

Melanie reached for her nightstand and picked up a foil packet. "I found it on the living-room floor where you dumped out your wallet."

Sam fumbled with the wrapper before getting it open.

"Let me," she said. She unrolled the little disk down his thickness. She could barely breathe, feeling his throbbing length in her hands, wanting him.

Then she mounted him, guiding his hardness into her. Slowly, she took him in, looking at his handsome face, until he filled her totally, completely.

She closed her eyes and began to slowly move up and down.

She was driving him mad. His hands fisted in the sheets as he tried to control himself until she was ready, too.

He'd never seen a more beautiful woman, a

woman so intent on pleasing him, taking pleasure herself. He reached for her breasts, playing with her nipples, squeezing, pulling until she groaned in enjoyment.

When he could stand no more, he pinned her under him, plunging into her as if he couldn't get enough. She met his every thrust, driving her body against his, until they both cried out in release.

They slept in each other's arms until they heard loud pounding on the front door, and male voices calling Melanie's name.

Melanie and Sam scrambled out of bed. Since Sam's clothes were hanging on pegs by the front door, he picked up the bath towel on the floor, and wrapped it around his waist.

"What's going on?" he asked.

"I don't have a clue," Melanie replied, hurrying to the door, wrapping a comforter around her. Sam followed to see if there was anything he could do.

She looked out the front window. "It's Dad and my brothers."

Sam hurriedly grabbed his pants and slid into them, just as Melanie swung open the front door.

"What's wrong? Where's Kyle?" Melanie's heart pounded violently.

Her father looked distraught. "He's missing."

"Missing?" Her voice was getting as high as her heart rate.

Brian hurried in. "We've already looked in the obvious places." Brian looked as bad as her father.

"Keep looking...please!" She turned around and bumped into Sam. "I have to get dressed."

Jack rushed into the room. His eyes were bleary and he was wet, like he'd tramped through the snow. "We've looked everywhere we could think of, and we called some of his friends. He isn't around. We need to look in the not-obvious places. We need more help."

Jack eyed Sam and his sister in their state of undress. Brian did the same. Sam shrugged into his shirt.

"It's still snowing hard out there." Melanie ran upstairs. "We have to find him."

"We have to keep calm," Sam said, but he doubted that would be possible. Everyone under this roof, including him, was already worried sick about Kyle. Sam knew they would have to push their worries aside and think rationally.

There was silence in the room as the three men stared at Sam. They were dripping snow and water onto Melanie's carpet, the same carpet on which they'd made love last night.

"I'll help find him." Sam sat on the floor and put his socks on, the same socks he'd worn all day yesterday. "Ed, what time did you realize that Kyle was missing?"

"About ten."

"What time is it now?" Sam asked.

"Almost noon." Brian's face was grim.

"I didn't get much sleep last night," Sam explained. "I slept in."

"We figured that out already." Jack raised an eyebrow.

Realizing that the conversation had drifted toward his relationship with Melanie, Sam stood and faced the two brothers. "Is there anything the two of you would like to ask me that probably isn't any of your business?"

Brian held up his hand like a traffic cop. "Melanie?"

Melanie ran back down the stairs, fully dressed. "Sam's right. It's none of your business. Now let's go and find Kyle."

"We need a plan," Sam said. "We should fan out from Ed's house, each of us taking a direction. I'm assuming he's on foot, right? I mean, he doesn't have access to a snowmobile or an ATV or anything like that, does he?"

"No," Ed said.

"So we have to figure out where he'd be

going," Sam said. "How about Hawk's Roost? Or the hockey rink at the high school? Or Tucker's farm where we had that play-off game."

"I'll take The Roost," Brian said. "Although there's no way he could walk all that way on foot."

"I'll take the high school," said Jack. "And the garage."

Ed nodded. "That leaves the Tucker place for me."

"I'll go to…oh, I don't know," Melanie said. "I can't think. Maybe his friend's Bobby's house."

"We already called Bobby's. He wasn't there," Ed said.

"I'll try again," she said, pulling her keys out of a drawer.

"I'll go with Melanie," Sam said. "We'll double back to Ed's house and see if he's returned. Keep in touch by cell."

A million things went through Melanie's mind, including the fact that there were a lot of strangers in town for the Snow Festival. She tried to calm her pumping heart. Kyle knew better than to talk to strangers or get into a car with anyone. He knew to scream and run like the wind if someone was bothering him.

Then again, he knew better than to leave his grandfather's house without telling anyone where he was going.

"What was he thinking? Where would he go?" Melanie's hands were shaking and she was on the brink of tears.

"I think I'd better drive," Sam said.

Melanie nodded and tossed him the keys. They both scraped the snow and ice off her car so they could hurry.

Kyle wasn't at Bobby's. He wasn't at Ed's. He wasn't at the garage. As they drove around, cell phone calls came in from her brothers and her father. No Kyle.

She called her father back on speaker so Sam could hear the conversation. "Dad, did Kyle hear the siren last night?"

"Yes. He was all worried. I had to call Bob McNeil at the firehouse because Kyle wouldn't let it go. When I found out that it was the transfer station again, I just told him that something hit a pole and knocked down some lines."

"That's fine, Dad. Did that ease his mind?"

"It did."

"Hey, Ed," Sam said. "Did he talk about anything else?"

"Just Santa Claus. He kept saying how he has to talk to Santa."

Melanie nodded. "Kyle starts talking about Santa Claus with the first snowfall. This year, Santa has been particularly on his mind."

"Then I think I know where he is," Sam said. "At the Santa Claus house at the village square."

"Oh, Sam! You could be right. Turn left at the next intersection, then a quick right," she pointed. "Dad, we'll call you if we find him."

Sam took a right by the bandstand and caught a flash of color by Santa's House.

"Does he have a yellow parka?" he asked.

"Yes. It's yellow and blue. Do you see him?"

"I think so. He's trying to walk over to the Santa Claus house."

"It's him!" Tears of joy and exasperation fell down her cheeks. She wiped them off with her mittens. "You were right."

"Go easy on him, Melanie. It's been tough on Kyle."

She sighed. "You're right. I was just—"

"Scared? I know." He reached for her hand. "I'll call Ed. You take care of your son."

He parked the car, and they walked across the square. There had to be three feet of snow on the ground, so it wasn't easy walking. Kyle spotted them, and looked guilty as hell, but at least he was adequately dressed.

"Kyle, you scared us all half to death," Melanie said, hugging him to her. She checked him for visible signs of frostbite, and he passed inspection.

"I'm sorry, Mom."

"You know better than to leave Grandpa's house and not tell anyone. Especially in a storm like this!"

"I know, but he was snoring, and I didn't want to wake him, and I had to see if Santa Claus was here, but he's not."

Melanie sat down next to him on the front porch of the little house.

"Santa's probably at the North Pole now, getting ready for the big day," Sam said.

"I have to talk to him."

The little boy looked like he had the weight of the world on his shoulders.

"There's still time to write him a letter," Sam suggested.

"I don't know how to spell all the words."

"Your mother and I could help you."

"Well…okay. I just wanted to tell Santa that I want to change what I want for Christmas."

"Okay," Melanie said, brushing snow from his hat.

Kyle turned to his mother, and then looked up at Sam.

"I want to tell Santa Claus that I know he can't bring my father back. That my dad died and is in heaven."

Melanie put her arm around her son. There were tears in her eyes.

"And I want to tell Santa Claus that I want Sam to be my new father."

Melanie looked up at Sam, her eyes wide.

"Will you write all that for me, Mom?" Kyle asked.

Melanie handed him a tissue. "Kyle, that's a difficult thing to ask Santa for."

"Why? Sam likes me, dontcha, Sam?" Kyle looked up at him, waiting for an answer, wiping his nose with the tissue.

"I sure do." And he did. He'd wished several times that he had a son like Kyle.

"And you like my mom, dontcha, Sam?"

"Kyle." Melanie straightened the ties on her son's hood. "I don't think you should ask such a question."

"Yes, Kyle. I like your mom."

I love your mom. Sam couldn't believe how easy it was to admit that to himself.

But how could he tell Melanie when he knew he'd be leaving soon?

Kyle grinned. He hugged his mother. "Good. Then *I'm* going to write a letter to Santa." Standing up, he hugged Sam, and Sam felt a rush of happiness and contentment that started in his heart and radiated out through his entire body.

If only things were that simple.

"Let's go," Kyle said. "I figure I'm going to be grounded, so I might as well write my letter to Santa right now. Christmas isn't far away, you know."

"You're right that you're going to be grounded, Kyle, and you're right that Christmas isn't far away," Melanie said. "And you've been naughty by running out on Grandpa. Bad timing on your part."

"I know, Mom."

"Get in the car, mister," Melanie said sternly.

Kyle started running toward the car, following the footprints they had already made.

Melanie and Sam just looked at each other. They both shook their heads.

Melanie said. "I'm sorry, Sam."

"What for?"

"Kyle's questions must be uncomfortable for you."

"He's just a boy." Sam brushed some snow from Melanie's shoulders. "Everything's so straightforward and uncomplicated. Kyle wants a father, and he picked me. I'm honored."

She pushed her hair back from her face. "Soon

you'll be leaving town, and I don't want Kyle to be hurt by another loss. I should have prepared him more."

"I guess," Sam said, a dull ache settling in his chest. If Melanie didn't want him here, there was nothing keeping him in Hawk's Lake.

Nothing except the woman and six-year-old boy he'd grown to love.

Chapter Fourteen

Melanie got to the garage at the crack of dawn the next day, intent on getting some work done so she could spend the afternoon doing her Christmas shopping.

No one was in the office when the phone rang, so she answered it.

"Hawk's Garage. Melanie speaking."

"Hi, Melanie. It's Tom Hyland. How's my Franklin coming along?"

"It's almost done, Tom. You can have it after the first of the year."

"How does it look?" he asked.

"It's a beauty, if I say so myself." Melanie was

proud of how the Franklin was progressing. "It's fit for a museum."

"I just might donate it or loan it out. And I can't wait to see it. I'm glad Sam told me about you."

"Sam who?"

"Sam LeDoux—you know, the ex-hockey player. Oh, shoot. I was supposed to keep that a secret."

"Why the big secret?"

"I haven't a clue."

Well, she did. Sam had gotten her the prestigious job. But why on earth would he do that?

Because he'd felt guilty.

For a second, Melanie was disappointed. She'd wanted to get jobs on her own merit and reputation. And yet she couldn't be too upset, given Sam's intentions.

"Uh...don't worry, Tom. I already know," she said to let him off the hook.

They said their goodbyes and hung up. Just then, Sam entered the garage bearing coffee and bakery boxes. "Thought you might be hungry."

"Sam, did you send work my way during the past year?" she asked, arms crossed.

"Work? As in cars?"

"Yes, as in cars." She tried to be stern. "As in Tom Hyland."

He set the coffee and boxes down on her toolbox. "I did tell Tom about you. He's a friend of mine." He handed her a cup of coffee. "Now before you say anything, I just wanted to help you and Kyle."

She thought about that for a minute, about his concern and consideration for her family. "I should probably thank you."

"That's not necessary. I wanted to do it. But I'm getting the idea that you aren't all that happy about it."

"I thought I'd gotten the work based on my own reputation," she said.

"You did. The East coast already knew about you. I just told a couple of friends on the West coast."

"What about the roadster? Did you have anything to do with that?" She pointed to the car in the corner of the garage.

"Another friend."

She walked closer to him, wrapped her arms around his neck and hugged him. "You are a very sweet man. Do you know that?"

"Keep telling me," he said, slanting his mouth over hers.

"I'll tell you again tonight, at the Snow Ball."

The Snow Ball at the Moose Lodge marked the end of the Snow Festival, and the whole town turned out for a buffet dinner and dancing. The kids would receive gifts, and attending would be the last of Sam's duties as grand marshal.

"I'll pick you and Kyle up at seven o'clock," he said.

She was looking forward to getting dressed up. She hadn't done that in a long time. Yet it made her sad. It would be one of their last times together before Christmas.

She'd miss him terribly, but she vowed to move on. She'd done it before, and she could do it again.

"We'll be ready," she said.

The Moose Lodge was transformed into a glittering and twinkling Christmas wonderland. Icicle lights dripped from every corner of the room. A big Christmas tree was left of the stage and a sign noted that it was decorated with ornaments made by the students of the grammar school. A mirrored ball rotated in the center of the ceiling, sending out colored patches of light circulating around the room.

Melanie looked spectacular in a dark green velvet dress that showed off her eyes and clung in the right places, and Sam vowed to make this an evening that she'd never forget. His lips grazed her neck as he led her to the dance floor. "You smell delicious."

"Gardenia."

"I know."

They danced two slow dances together, and Sam was just about to kiss her when Cal Lippert called his name. "This should be my last duty as grand marshal," he said to Melanie before following Cal to the stage where the Happy Hunters band were just finishing a loud polka.

The lead singer handed the microphone to Cal, who waited for the crowd to quiet down. "I'd like to extend our warmest gratitude to Samuel LeDoux for his assistance to the people of Hawk's Lake and their neighbors. For two years in a row, Sam helped out during an ice storm and blizzard." The mayor turned to Sam. "Sam, we'd love to have you back for a third year, but without the storm, please."

Sam laughed as Cal and the crowd clapped. Cal invited Sam to say a few words, but he declined with a polite bow.

He wanted to dance with Melanie.

But he wasn't going to get that chance. Someone handed him an index card, and Cal handed him the microphone.

Sam studied the typed message, then read from the card. "Santa is busy at the North Pole getting ready for his big day, so he's asked the Hawk's Lake Fire Department Ladies Auxiliary to help him pass out some early gifts for our young people."

A big cheer went up from the crowd. The youngsters were already sitting around the Christmas tree ogling the colorfully wrapped presents. The only thing that stopped the kids from tearing into them was the watchful eye of their parents and the auxiliary.

The children were starting to squirm, so Sam read quickly. "Boys and girls, when your name is called, go to the person who has called your name, and she will help you find your gifts."

Immediately they sat like little statues around the tree. Sam tried not to laugh.

Sam watched Melanie, a member of the Auxiliary, take the children to find their gifts under the tree. She floated in her emerald gown. He could watch her all day and night.

But he couldn't. The parents of Emily Farley came over to talk to him.

Mrs. Farley put a hand on Sam's arm. "Thank you so much for getting the presents for Emily," she whispered. "I know you are her Secret Santa."

Sam shrugged. "Why, I don't know what you mean, Mrs.—"

"Farley. Linda Farley. And this is my husband Steve."

Sam shook the man's hand.

"I'd like to add my thanks, Mr. LeDoux. It'll be a wonderful holiday for Emily. And I—we just couldn't—"

Steve's voice cracked, and Sam could only imagine what he was feeling. Sam grabbed his shoulder. "Merry Christmas."

Just then Melanie appeared. "Hello. Am I interrupting something?"

"Melanie, this is Linda and Steve Farley. They seem to think I gave their daughter presents."

Melanie smiled. "I just helped Emily pick out her stocking." She pointed to the smiling little girl sitting under the big Christmas tree on the side of the hall.

Sam rubbed his chin. "No. She doesn't look familiar to me. You must have the wrong person. Excuse us, please." He took Melanie's hand. "I promised to dance all night with this beautiful lady."

Sam shook their hands again, then escorted Melanie to the dance floor.

"I don't think they believed you," Melanie

said. "And you did another nice thing that I know about."

"What do you mean?"

"You saw to it that Emily had gifts here tonight. The coordinator of the gift committee for the auxiliary told me that you'd called to give them Emily's name, and that she might be here tonight and to make sure something was here for her."

He smiled.

Melanie stood on her toes and gave him the sweetest kiss he'd ever received. "You're a wonderful, thoughtful man."

"Oh, you know that I can't take all·the credit, Mel. The lady that I talked to said that you had *already* submitted Emily's name."

Before she could respond, he pulled her toward him and returned her kiss.

He just couldn't get enough of her sweet kisses. How he'd miss them…

What was he thinking? He couldn't leave Hawk's Lake. Not the way he felt about Melanie. He loved her. He thought she loved him, too, but he didn't know for sure.

He'd give up his Red Cross job, and get a job here in town. He had good investments that were paying off, and had a lot of money saved

he could live off of. They could be together—
they could be a family.

How could it not work out?

Melanie was helping to cut a big cake in the
shape of a snowman family. Sam was talking to
Ed and Melanie's brothers when his cell phone
rang. Glancing at the number, he didn't recog-
nize the number, but it was long-distance. He
stepped away from the crowd.

"This is Sam LeDoux."

"Mr. LeDoux, my name is Ron Whitney. I'm
the director of emergency management for New
York State. Did I catch you at a bad time?"

"Only if you're going to tell me that I'm
needed somewhere. I was hoping for a nice,
peaceful Christmas." He looked over at Melanie.
She had a big smile on her face and looked beautiful tonight, glowing and happy. He couldn't
wait until she was back in his arms again. "What
can I do for you?"

Sam held his breath, dreading the response.
It had to be important to get a call on a Saturday night.

"I've heard about what you've done for Hawk's
Lake—two years in a row. Several residents of
the area have called my office, including Mayor

Lippert. I must admit that I've also talked to the Red Cross about you."

Sam waited for him to get to the point. Noticing Melanie looking at him, he waved, and she waved back. Then she blew him a kiss, and several heads turned toward him.

"...and to that end, we'd like to offer you the job of area coordinator and director of emergency training for the upstate New York district."

Sam snapped to attention. "Sorry...uh... Ron. I was distracted for a moment. Could you repeat that?"

He laughed. "We'd like to establish, and are prepared to fund, a training facility for emergency response. We'd like you to oversee the entire operation and be the coordinator of training, hire a staff, etcetera. If you are interested, we can set up a time to meet in my office in Albany. We can discuss the preliminary details and salary requirements then."

Sam couldn't believe his good fortune. "Where do you plan on locating the facility?"

"Wherever you think. We have people on staff who can—"

"I think that Hawk's Lake would be a perfect area."

"Fine with me."

Sam grinned. This couldn't be any more perfect. "Ron, I'd like to thank you for your offer. I'm definitely interested."

They arranged to meet after the holidays.

Sam couldn't wait to tell Melanie. What luck. He could train others in emergency management, and he wouldn't have to leave Hawk's Lake. His mind was already reeling with plans and courses that would be needed. He could add EMT certification, and...

He pushed the job offer to the back of his mind. Right now, the Happy Hunters were playing a danceable Christmas tune, and it looked like Melanie was heading his way. The way his luck was running, they would meet halfway, on the dance floor.

"Oh Sam, that's a wonderful tribute to you!" Melanie lit up like a Christmas tree when he told her.

"Does that mean that all the counties in New York would send trainees here?"

He nodded, thinking that Ron Whitney was *his* Secret Santa. Everything was falling into place. There was only one piece that was missing, and that piece was Melanie.

"Are you going to accept the job?"

He met her gaze. "I don't know yet."

He tried to read her face, but she was looking away, toward the Christmas tree, then at the band. She was looking everywhere but at him. He'd thought that she'd be happier. He'd thought that she'd leap into his arms and scream with joy, for heaven's sake.

Didn't she want him to stay in Hawk's Lake?

"Do you want me to take the job?" he finally asked.

"It's entirely up to you, Sam. You have to make this decision on your own. This is your life, your career, and you have to be happy. My opinion shouldn't matter."

She bit down on her lower lip, as if she were trying to keep her feelings in check. He held out his arms, and they danced again.

It wasn't what she'd said that tweaked him—it was what she hadn't said.

Over the next few days, Melanie went shopping, wrapped presents, decorated and put the finishing touches on the Phaeton.

Her brothers, Sam, and Kyle played hockey daily on the frozen lake. Others, young and old, joined them as the word got out that there was a continuous game.

Finally, it was two o'clock in the afternoon

on Christmas Eve. The table was set and everything looked festive and just perfect.

Sam looked handsome in a cranberry golf shirt and a pair of khaki pants. Kyle was dressed almost identically.

Royal Catering had come and gone and the smells wafting from the kitchen were delicious. They'd left typed instructions for what to do and when. All Melanie had to do was take the serving dishes from the stove and put them on the table.

Everyone was watching *Miracle on 34th Street*. Actually, they were mostly talking and munching on snacks. Sam had his arm around Kyle as they sat on the couch and shared a bowl of popcorn.

Just watching Sam, Melanie thought her heart would burst with happiness. But she was nervous, too. When she found the right time, she was going to tell Sam she loved him and ask him to take the job and stay.

When Sam motioned for her to go to the kitchen, she froze. Was something burning?

She ran into the room and grabbed some potholders to open the stove. All looked well.

Strong arms wrapped around her from behind. When she faced him, Sam's lips descended on hers. The kiss was genuine and passionate, strong and yet gentle.

She'd been so worried about Kyle's ability to deal with Sam leaving Hawk's Lake that she'd forgot to convince herself that she could handle it, too.

Later that night, after a delicious holiday dinner, Hawk's Roost was finally quiet.

Ed had turned in. Brian and Jack hadn't yet returned from driving their dates home.

As she wiped the table off and Sam dried the last coffee cup, she decided that it was a wonderful Christmas Eve—full of laughter, music and much Christmas cheer. Relatives and friends stopped by all evening, laden with presents and cookies.

Sam and Melanie had tucked Kyle into bed earlier, heard his prayers and assured him that Santa Claus had received his most recent letter.

Sam hung the damp dish towel over the bar on the stove, took her hand, and they walked into the living room. He sat on the couch in front of the Christmas tree and poured two glasses of wine.

Instead of joining him on the couch, Melanie stood at the window looking out at the gently falling snow, rehearsing what she wanted to say to Sam.

"What are you thinking about, Melanie?"

It was the perfect opportunity to tell him that she loved him with all of her heart. Instead she said, "I'm thinking about how things change. About how angry I used to be, and how much I've come to—"

Melanie turned, wanting to see Sam's face before she went on.

But Sam was kneeling before her. Her eyes opened wide when he took her hands in his.

"Sam?"

"Melanie, I love you, and I love Kyle as if he were my own son. Marry me, and I promise to dedicate my life to making you happy."

Tears flooded her eyes, then trailed slowly down her cheeks. "Oh, Sam! I love you, too!"

"I was hoping you'd say that." He kissed her. "I want that new job. I want to stay here in Hawk's Lake and be a father to Kyle and a husband to you."

"But what if the Red Cross needs you?" Melanie took his hand. "I've seen you at work, and you are outstanding at what you do. If you're needed somewhere, you should go. You just have to promise me that you'll take of yourself and phone home all the time."

"I don't know if I want to leave you—ever.

Besides, Hawk's Lake is the perfect place to raise a bunch of kids."

"A bunch of kids?" Her eyes took on a dreamy quality.

"However many we want," he said. "If that's okay with you."

She launched herself into his arms.

"Yes! I'd love more children with you. Oh, Sam! Of course I'll marry you."

He pulled her onto him for several more kisses. "Tell me you love me again."

"I love you. I always will." She kissed him with all the passion and love in her heart.

"Sam, remember when you asked me what I'd like for Christmas, and I didn't answer?"

"Yes."

She gazed at him, tears of happiness in her eyes. "This was my wish."

He nuzzled her neck. "I'm such a good Secret Santa!"

The grandfather clock chimed. It was midnight. Christmas Day.

"Merry Christmas, Melanie."

"*Joyeux Noël*, Sam."

As they embraced by the glittering Christmas tree, Melanie knew for certain that Christmas wishes definitely did come true.

Epilogue

Kyle woke up on Christmas morning and just knew that he was going to get his Christmas wish. He'd written a perfect letter to Santa and spelled all the words right.

He didn't know how he was going to get his present, but he knew Santa wouldn't let him down.

He ran to the great room and stopped when he looked under the tree. Sam was sleeping between the gifts. He had a big red bow on his forehead and a card in his hand.

Kyle tiptoed quietly over to Sam and slowly pulled the card from Sam's hand.

"To Kyle Bennett. From Santa Claus." Kyle let out a hoot. "Awesome!"

Sam opened his eyes and held out his arms. Kyle made a flying leap to Sam's chest and gave him a big hug.

From the doorway, Melanie saw the glow on her son's happy face, and the equally joyful face of the man she loved, and she knew that this was her best Christmas ever.

* * * * *

HOMETOWN HEARTS ♥

YES! Please send me **The Hometown Hearts Collection** in Larger Print. This collection begins with 3 FREE books and 2 FREE gifts in the first shipment. Along with my 3 free books, I'll also get the next 4 books from the Hometown Hearts Collection, in LARGER PRINT, which I may either return and owe nothing, or keep for the low price of $4.99 U.S./ $5.89 CDN each plus $2.99 for shipping and handling per shipment*. If I decide to continue, about once a month for 8 months I will get 6 or 7 more books, but will only need to pay for 4. That means 2 or 3 books in every shipment will be FREE! If I decide to keep the entire collection, I'll have paid for only 32 books because 19 books are FREE! I understand that accepting the 3 free books and gifts places me under no obligation to buy anything. I can always return a shipment and cancel at any time. My free books and gifts are mine to keep no matter what I decide.

262 HCN 3432 462 HCN 3432

Name	(PLEASE PRINT)	
Address		Apt. #
City	State/Prov.	Zip/Postal Code

Signature (if under 18, a parent or guardian must sign)

Mail to the **Reader Service:**
IN U.S.A.: P.O. Box 1867, Buffalo, NY. 14240-1867
IN CANADA: P.O. Box 609, Fort Erie, Ontario L2A 5X3

Get 2 Free Books,
Plus 2 Free Gifts—
just for trying the
Reader Service!

Get 2 Free Books,
Plus 2 Free Gifts—
just for trying the Reader Service!

Get 2 Free Books,
Plus 2 Free Gifts—
just for trying the
Reader Service!

HARLEQUIN *super romance*

YES! Please send me 2 FREE LARGER-PRINT Harlequin® Superromance® novels and my 2 FREE gifts (gifts are worth about $10 retail). After receiving them, if I don't wish to receive any more books, I can return the shipping statement marked "cancel." If I don't cancel, I will receive 4 brand-new novels every month and be billed just $6.19 per book in the U.S. or $6.49 per book in Canada. That's a savings of at least 11% off the cover price! It's quite a bargain! Shipping and handling is just 50¢ per book in the U.S. or 75¢ per book in Canada.* I understand that accepting the 2 free books and gifts places me under no obligation to buy anything. I can always return a shipment and cancel at any time. The free books and gifts are mine to keep no matter what I decide.

132/332 HDN GLWS

Name _____ (PLEASE PRINT) _____

Address _____ Apt. # _____

City _____ State/Prov. _____ Zip/Postal Code _____

Signature (if under 18, a parent or guardian must sign) _____

Mail to the **Reader Service:**
IN U.S.A.: P.O. Box 1341, Buffalo, NY 14240-8531
IN CANADA: P.O. Box 603, Fort Erie, Ontario L2A 5X3

Want to try two free books from another line?
Call 1-800-873-8635 today or visit www.ReaderService.com.

* Terms and prices subject to change without notice. Prices do not include applicable taxes. Sales tax applicable in N.Y. Canadian residents will be charged applicable taxes. Offer not valid in Quebec. This offer is limited to one order per household. Books received may not be as shown. Not valid for current subscribers to Harlequin Superromance Larger-Print books. All orders subject to approval. Credit or debit balances in a customer's account(s) may be offset by any other outstanding balance owed by or to the customer. Please allow 4 to 6 weeks for delivery. Offer available while quantities last.

Your Privacy—The Reader Service is committed to protecting your privacy. Our Privacy Policy is available online at www.ReaderService.com or upon request from the Reader Service.

We make a portion of our mailing list available to reputable third parties that offer products we believe may interest you. If you prefer that we not exchange your name with third parties, or if you wish to clarify or modify your communication preferences, please visit us at www.ReaderService.com/consumerschoice or write to us at Reader Service Preference Service, P.O. Box 9062, Buffalo, NY 14240-9062. Include your complete name and address.

HSRLP17R

Get 2 Free Books,
Plus 2 Free Gifts—
just for trying the Reader Service!

Get 2 Free Books,
Plus 2 Free Gifts -

just for
trying the
*Reader
Service!*